BHAUNRI

A Novel

Anukrti Upadhyay

FOURTH ESTATE • *New Delhi*

First published in India in 2019 by Fourth Estate
An imprint of HarperCollins *Publishers*
A-75, Sector 57, Noida, Uttar Pradesh 201301, India
www.harpercollins.co.in

2 4 6 8 10 9 7 5 3 1

P-ISBN: 978-93-5357-003-3
E-ISBN: 978-93-5357-004-0

The typeface used in the title of this book has been created in collaboration with Gond tattoo tribal artists Ram Keli, Sunita and Sumitra from Chhattisgarh as part of The Typecraft Initiative (typecraftinitiative.org) to help revive and promote Indian culture through the digital medium.

Typeset in 10.5/16.3 Scala at
Manipal Digital Systems, Manipal

Printed and bound at
Thomson Press (India) Ltd

This book is produced from independently certified FSC® paper to ensure responsible forest management.

To you, for whom I pressed
a thorn to my aching breast

I

BHAUNRI WAS TALL FOR her age. Dark-skinned, with the sun-bleached hair of a nomad, startling cat-like eyes in her shadowy face, she was always noticeable among the group of girls and boys with whom she grazed her mother's goats. As she grew into womanhood, she took to walking with her long neck held taut, her head slightly bent, as if she were balancing a pair of earthen pots on her head.

Bhaunri belonged to the desert clan of Gadoliya Lohars. Her father, a nomadic blacksmith, used to traverse the desert in his ox cart, making and repairing pots and pans, hoes and scythes. After marrying Bhaunri's mother, he had pitched camp in a small village which had no resident blacksmith. The village was in a desert oasis, an oasis so small that its perennial lake did not figure in the state's maps. At his wife's advice, he had petitioned the District Collector for land to settle down in the village. The administration was keen to control the free movement of nomads across the Thar desert, for neither the nomads nor the desert respected the blood-soaked borders drawn between the two nations. Bhaunri's father's request was granted after some persuasion, which required him to sell his cart, his pair of oxen and his wife's silver anklets. He regretted the loss of his cart, the symbol of his clan and his craft, but his wife did not mind losing her best piece of jewellery. A beauty with curved brows and the undulating gait of a she-camel, she was not from the clan of blacksmiths; she was from the tribe of Gujjars who kept cattle and farmed. Gujjars were semi-nomadic, and though they had pretensions of being better than desert nomads like the Lohars, in truth they followed similar traditions and were treated no differently by the upper-caste folk. 'Don't mourn, my husband. The sound grain makes in a ripe ear of millet is sweeter to me than any anklet,' she said to her husband and set about helping him build a mud house on a part of the land. The rest of the land she farmed. No longer a traveller, Bhaunri's father set up a forge at the doorstep of his house to make and repair iron implements. He taught his children his craft too, and Bhaunri learnt to work the bellows and wield a hammer at his forge along with her brothers. She also helped her mother cook, fetch water and tend to the field and goats. But she dreamt alone, flowing inwards like a subterranean river in the desert, occasionally flashing in the sun, nourishing herself from unseen sources.

Bhaunri had been married to a young blacksmith when she was a little girl, though she still lived in her father's home. Her mother sometimes mentioned her marriage. 'The panch of your father's community fixed it,' her mother would complain. 'Your father did not meet your father-in-law before the match was made, never smoked his hookah or offered him tobacco. Your in-laws have never darkened our door. Even on your wedding day, the menfolk from your in-laws' clan came to the village temple for the ceremony. This isn't the way marriages are supposed to happen.' She would shake her head, setting the numerous silver earrings covering her ear aquiver. Bhaunri's own memories of the event were vague. She remembered being dressed in stiff, new clothes one afternoon, along with a number of other little boys and girls from the village. She also remembered eating handfuls of the sticky sweet distributed at the shrine of Kalika Mai, and the resounding slap from her mother when she broke one of the eleven ritual threads tied to her father's house-door. The memory of that afternoon had grown faint with time. So when, at sixteen, she overheard her mother and father discussing her departure to her husband's home, half a day's journey from her village, she was puzzled. In that childhood memory, there hadn't been a husband.

Born after four boys, Bhaunri was the only daughter in her father's family. She had a special place in her mother's heart, this late-arriving, last-born child. 'The womb-wiper', her mother called her – one who is last to emerge from a fecund womb – and gazed at her strong, well-formed body with pride. Unlike the upper-caste folk who wore long faces when a girl was born to them, sometimes bribing the midwives to smother the baby or feed her opium, Lohars did not mind daughters. In fact, daughters were welcome. They worked at the family forge and fetched a good bride-price at the time of marriage. But Bhaunri's mother had steadfastly refused a bride-price for her daughter. 'I will take Bhaunri in my arms and jump into the baoli,' she had threatened when her husband was tempted by the large sums offered for their sturdy little girl. 'I will curse your seven succeeding generations! You won't have anyone to give comfort to the living or water to the dead if you sell my daughter!'

Bhaunri's father had backed off; he knew that his wife's threats were not empty. Her own family had sold her to an old man, a Gujjar chieftain with a hundred heads of cattle, some land, and four children from a previous wife. 'He was as limp as a wilted stalk of millet, and as dry,' Bhaunri had often heard her mother say. One day, a young Lohar had come to the old Gujjar's homestead. He wanted to buy a pair of bullocks for his cart. Bhaunri's mother had shown him the animals. She handled the cattle with ease, holding back frolicking yearlings and pushing forward the heavy, ponderous older bulls for inspection. The Lohar had marvelled at her strength.

Later, she had given him bajra roti to eat, with buttermilk and chutney made from hot red chillies and garlic.

The old Gujjar had noticed the way his bride's gaze lingered on the young Lohar as he squatted smoking a hookah, his blacksmith's arms relaxed, the muscles in his thighs taut under the length of coarse cotton that he wore. The desert's rigid code of hospitality demanded that a guest could never be turned away. Besides, he did not wish to lose a potential customer. The Gujjar was shrewd, he had lived and thrived in the desert's hardships for many years. He acted quickly. Taking a pitcher full of water, he poured it over the bedclothes stacked in the small storehouse and hung them out on the drying-rope. Next, he tethered a couple of his goats in the inner courtyard. 'Unfortunately,' he said to the Lohar, his palms joined, his eyes gleaming, 'I have no bed to offer to you tonight. You see, the woman has foolishly washed all the bedding at the same time. She has little sense and is often quarrelsome. But I don't blame her – she is a mere woman, thoughtless and easily distracted. You are welcome to sleep on my cot in the courtyard, but there are all these sick goats here tonight. The Mother Goddess's plague has been rampant around here and I need to nurse them myself.'

'Please put yourself at ease about me,' the young Lohar answered. 'I will be quite comfortable in my cart. I am used to sleeping in it.'

After the Lohar retreated to his cart, the wily Gujjar placed his own string cot in the courtyard near the door. He slept lightly and would hear if his wife stepped out of the house. He was satisfied that, with him guarding the door, she would not be able to secretly leave for a rendezvous with the young guest. Bhaunri's mother watched his stratagem impassively. At midnight, she tied bits of cloth around her heavy anklets to deaden their jangling, lifted her room's thatched roof, and slipped out like a dhaman snake.

The Lohar's cart was at some distance from the house, right where the village receded into the desert. She shook the soundly sleeping Lohar by the shoulder. 'I am withering, like a jasmine flower withers without sweet water,' she said, as she stood holding the pole of his cart, the meagre moon outlining her in flowing, curving lines against the desert's expanse. 'Take me with you. I will work your forge and cook your meals and bear your children.' The Lohar gazed at the lightning eyes of the woman before him, her bare arms gleaming like acacia branches, her bosom, bound in the kurti, heaving. Her smell, like that of the dunes and desert breeze, enveloped him. 'If you are a man born of a woman,' she challenged, 'take me.' She was older than him, and her husband was a rich man, a panch of the Gujjar community. Besides, he was the Lohar's host too; the young blacksmith had eaten the bread and salt of his household. But he was captivated. He did not care if he broke the covenant of hospitality or incurred the hostility of a powerful man. This was the woman for him. He left before dawn broke – without the new bullocks he needed for his cart, but with a wife he wanted keenly.

Bhaunri's mother's family was furious. Her brothers set out to find the pair as soon as they learnt of her elopement. They eventually traced her to the village where the Lohar had set up camp. 'Why would you leave your husband's house?' they railed at the young woman. 'And that too for a man with no settled home, who lives like a lonely, outcast camel in the desert.' Bhaunri's mother was unfazed. 'I am not a high-caste woman. I couldn't stay in the home of a man who is husband only in name and die of frustration,' she retorted. 'I can earn my keep anywhere. I will follow my hivda, not another's tukda.' 'You think the world of your own heart and dare despise the bread of your husband's home? You ate fine grain and butter there. This pauper will not be able to give you even the coarsest millet,' they shouted. Bhaunri's mother would have shoved them out of the camp, but the Lohar remained calm. He agreed to pay back the bride-price to the old Gujjar together with the fine which he demanded and settle the whole matter with her family and her ex-husband.

'She has not borne me a single child, male or female,' the Gujjar said in the council he had summoned to settle the dispute. 'One tends the vine for fruit.' The elders of the community nodded in agreement, but Bhaunri's mother was livid. 'It's not I who am fruitless. Ask the gardener whether he sowed any seed,' she said loudly enough for all to hear. 'In fact, I should be paid harjana for the nights I spent writhing like a fish out of water by his side.' The assembled men laughed and the women bit their tongues at her tartness but the elders of the clan decreed that the fine must be paid. 'Don't pay,' Bhaunri's mother said to her new husband. 'Don't buy me.' 'It is not your price that I'm paying. I am giving the old man money to buy a bed-warmer,' he said laughing, and gave away all his savings. To this day, Bhaunri's mother taunted the Lohar for caving in. 'He is a big soorma, but he paid a fine without shaking his horns or tail to an old, impotent man who claimed I was barren – and that, when my womb was already cradling his own seed,' she would say. 'But remember, Dhola, you did not buy me. I came of my own free will.' Bhaunri would catch the curve of a half-smile behind her father's moustache as he'd answer, 'Of course I didn't buy you, fortunate one, I sold myself to you.' And Bhaunri's mother's shining eyes would rest on her husband for a long moment.

NOT LONG AFTER her parents began discussing her bidai, a travelling barber brought a message from Bhaunri's husband's family. He also brought finery and ornaments for Bhaunri. 'These are gifts for your girl from her mother-in-law. Be prepared,' he said. 'Our lada will come for his bride soon.' After drinking buttermilk and delivering the message to Bhaunri's father and mother, he toured the village. He gave haircuts and shaves and told anyone willing to give him an ear about Bhaunri's wealthy in-laws. 'They have sent sixteen types of ornaments for the girl, all in the old king's silver, not the new gilt stuff. They eat fresh goat meat, and there is milk to soak your tikkad morning, noon and night. And the mother-in-law is like a cow, loving and simple. They have a pakka house, and the old family cart handed down by their ancestors is painted twice a year and decorated with dhaal, ghunghar and patti of real silver,' he announced to his customers as he vigorously massaged their heads or lathered their chins. 'They live like Rajputs. Your girl will have the life of a queen. She will never need to lift a hammer or blow into the bellows again.'

People in the village heard him with disbelief. How could Bhaunri, that daughter of Lohars, tall like a camel and dark like the clouds of Ashadh, be so lucky? Bhaunri's mother was incredulous too, not because she thought her daughter undeserving but because, in her experience, it was seldom that the deserving got their due. She held the ornaments sent by Bhaunri's mother-in-law in her two hands to judge their cast and weight. To satisfy herself about the purity of the silver, she took them to a jeweller in the market-town two hours away. 'There's no doubt about their purity,' the jeweller pronounced after rubbing each of them carefully on the black kasauti stone. 'The items are all pure silver. Solid too. Heavy, valuable. None of the hollow moulds or cheap castings so common nowadays,' he added, handing them back to Bhaunri's mother.

Bhaunri's mother returned to the village, more perplexed and suspicious than before. 'Why would they give so much?' she said to her husband that night. 'One or two things I could understand, but all ornaments from head to toe? After all, we are Lohars, not Brahmins or Baniyas. And she is not even the only daughter-in-law. There's another son, an older one. Something's wrong, I am sure.'

'Nothing's wrong,' Bhaunri's father said emphatically. 'Absolutely nothing except your head, which is filled to the brim with cow dung. Instead of rejoicing in your daughter's good fortune, you are being foolish, like a traveller who suspects an oasis to be a mirage.'

'If there's cow dung in my head, the creator has made yours with unyielding stones, my husband,' her mother retorted. 'I don't know just bridal songs but also the price of millet, whereas all you know is how to hammer and blow.'

She would not brook his authority if he wielded it like a hammer, only when he waved it like a flower-wand. She knew she worked harder than him. Besides looking after the household, she tended to the cattle, and the melons and vegetables she grew sold at a better price than his plough-edges and axe-blades and spade-heads. 'When someone does too much, it is a sign they are trying to dazzle your eyes with generosity and blind you to reality. Remember the saying – the deceiver is twice as polite as anyone else. You must find out more about these people to whom you are joining our Bhaunri for life. I won't send her to them unless you do.' Bhaunri's father grumbled, but gave in.

The inquiries revealed nothing to contradict the barber's glowing reports. Bhaunri's in-laws were indeed very well off. Her husband's family was among the first in their clan to break the nomadic vows of not living in a house or being part of a settled community. Bhaunri's father-in-law's father had convinced his clan to form a settlement and approach a local politician for a grant of land. He volunteered to mediate with the government and collected the thumbprints of most of his clansmen. When the government granted land to the clan, he usurped most of it, doling out a little money to them in exchange. Eventually, his clansmen farmed the land, which should have been theirs by right, as his tenant-farmers. 'You are better off like this,' he would say to them furrowing his brows, 'you don't have to face the endless troubles with Ameens and the Patwari, or worry about paying large sums to Sarkar Bahadur whether the crop dries up or is eaten by locusts.' Oddly, his dishonesty was not held against him. If anything, it enhanced his reputation of sagacity. 'He is crafty and wise like the upper-caste folk,' his clansmen said and appointed him their panch and arbitrator in disputes. They sought out his advice and held him in greater esteem than the priests at the shrine of Ramsha Pir. Though the village Bhaunri's in-laws lived in had Jats and Gujjars and other castes, such was the Lohar clan's standing that the village was named after them.

Lately, though, the family's prestige had declined somewhat. Bhaunri's father-in-law had closed his forge. 'He tours villages and market-towns, buying and selling goods like an ordinary Banjara, but he is said to make a lot of money. There is some rift between the father and son too, but that is bound to happen,' Bhaunri's father explained to her mother. 'A grown son and an able father are like two swords in one scabbard, sparks are bound to fly. The mother-in-law is known to be kind and gentle,' he added, 'and beautiful too, it is said – a samdhin worth having.' His eyes twinkled. Bhaunri's mother threw him a look. 'Take care, her old man might think the same about me.' 'If he does, God save him, for I won't lift a finger to help him when you tear him in two with your words!' Not much, however, could be learnt about the elder son. He wasn't married, or perhaps his wife was dead. 'Anyway, that's not the one Bhaunri is going to,' her father said.

Her husband, the younger son, was well known in the village. He had been to a big school in a nearby town, and had learnt enough to be able to write his name, add and subtract, and wear a shirt instead of the jhagga worn by village folk. He had broken away completely from the clan's traditional iron-craft and had set up a shop in the village selling all kinds of dry goods. 'But times have changed. New people can't live according to old ways,' Bhaunri's father said. 'And what does working with iron give these days anyway, now that things are made by machines? Only a pittance, and lungs filled with ashes and iron fillings. Besides, the boy works hard and is making money. He is also something of a banka gabru.' He smiled. 'Very fashionable and good looking. He looks more like a Jat than a Lohar. He is said to be rather inordinately fond of wrestling, and his dogs. But an akhada or dogs as a pastime are any day better than smoking tobacco or ganja and idling around the village, or worse,' he reasoned. 'One or two people mentioned his hot temper, but what do you expect from a young man like that? When there is strength in the body, the head heats up easily. You remember how hot-headed I was?' Bhaunri's mother smiled, 'Yes, I do, but you had me. If you were iron, I was flint.'

'Make no mistake, wife, Bhaunri is your daughter and mine. If you are flint, she is steel. This is a good match. She will be comfortable, she will eat wheat chapatis with cow milk and butter, and rest on a soft cotton mattress. Don't imagine snakes under every shade-tree.'

BHAUNRI HEARD THE conversation between her father and mother. There were Jats in her village. Though they were held to be only a notch above Lohars in the caste hierarchy by upper-caste families, their men and women were considered good-looking. Tall, fair-skinned and light-eyed, to her they resembled the smooth marble statues of gods that were brought from Jaipur when the new temple had been consecrated in the village. Her puzzlement about her husband gave way to curiosity and anticipation.

2

BHAUNRI'S MOTHER GAVE HER grudging consent for the bidai after Bhaunri's father visited her in-laws in their village and saw the fine house they lived in, and the fields and shop they owned, with his own eyes.

The morning of the day her husband was to come and take her away, Bhaunri's mother dressed her with care. She made her wear a red, wide-skirted ghaghra. The mirrors on her kanchali reflected the sun. A heavy borla was balanced on her forehead, silver chokers and coin-necklaces, stiff like the collars on the necks of bullock, chafed her long neck. Silver anklets, thick and twisted like the roots of an old banyan tree, hampered her gait. Her arms were covered from shoulder to wrist with white ivory bangles; she could not bend them with ease. But despite the discomfort, she admired the dull, white gleam and comforting weight of the silver on her dark body, and was not a little proud of these gifts sent by her unseen husband to adorn her.

Just before noon, her husband arrived with his uncle and cousins. He entered the house first. His tall, broad-shouldered form filled the doorframe. Bhaunri's breath caught as his shadow fell on her – she had never seen anyone as handsome as him. Instantaneously, she forgot that he was a stranger; she only remembered that he was her husband. For her part, Bhaunri's mother cast a sour look at her new, and only, son-in-law. Her heart twisted within her. He had come to claim her only daughter, and unless he nourished her heart with love, cherished her carefully, why should she part with the child of her womb? 'Men as good-looking as this one are always bad news,' she muttered.

Bhaunri's father laid out string cots, spread thick, cotton durries on them, and invited the guests to sit. She watched as the men settled on the cots and then turned her veil-less face towards the guests. 'Welcome, son-in-law,' she said in her ringing voice. 'You see I do not cover my face before you, for isn't a son-in-law like a son? And is there any need for a mother to cover her face in front of one who suckled at her breast?' The men listened in silence. Bhaunri handed them earthen pots filled with freshly churned buttermilk. 'I have taught Bhaunri everything,' her mother continued. 'She can cook a complete meal with two pods of sangari and a handful of lentils, she can birth a calf and ply a hammer, she can sing, dance. But,' her mother paused, and the scowl that had been hovering around her mouth ever since the entry of her guests finally appeared. 'But I have also taught her to strike and escape like a nagin if need be.'

Bhaunri's husband had heard about his mother-in-law from the barber, about her escape from her former husband's home. 'She is wilful,' the barber had said. 'Her husband's like her puppet. She knows some magic and can make difficult births easy, can cure children's ailments caused by the evil eye. The village folk speak of her with respect. All this has gone to the twice-bedded witch's head.' The barber had touched his ears in fear.

Bhaunri's husband rose from the cot and flexed the muscles in his neck and shoulders. 'Don't worry mother-in-law,' he said. 'Goga-ji's shrine in our village is famous in the entire district. We pray to him and are not afraid of snakes. Besides,' he added, 'the roof of our house is made of stone and cement, not thatch, so there is no danger of your daughter slipping out that way.' His clansmen sniggered. Even Bhaunri's father laughed.

Her mother turned away. 'I have said what I needed to say. I don't have time to bandy words or to stand around and giggle foolishly. Come, Bhaunri, we must prepare food for the guests.' Bhaunri followed her, casting a glance at her husband who still stood in the courtyard, his feet planted wide, proud like a male deer. She was certain she would never want to run away from him. At the entrance of the kitchen, her mother stopped and looked at her. 'Remember, girl,' she said, her voice audible all over the house. 'I did not stay with a man who did not please me. If hearts don't meet, bodies are but fleshly houses of sin.'

Bhaunri's mother fed her guests a sumptuous meal – thick, fresh maize bread, pats of pale butter made from buffalo milk, goat's meat cooked to tenderness with yoghurt and chillies, whole green chillies roasted on wood fire, and pearly-skinned onions. Bhaunri prepared sweet kheer with milk and rice, and served it in a large brass bowl to her husband, her eyes never leaving him as he ate. Her mother saw it, and her forehead tightened and her scowl deepened.

After the meal, Bhaunri's husband and his party sat in the courtyard, chatting with her father. Folk from the village came to meet him, but they found Bhaunri's groom rather taciturn. He spoke little and smiled even less, prompting the women to conclude he was close-natured, giving nothing away. 'He is ghunna too, just like our Bhaunri,' they said. 'Like bride, like groom. Ramsha Pir matched them well.' They admired his good looks and wondered aloud at Bhaunri's mother's ill temper amidst such blessings. 'How come only so few of you have come to fetch our Bhaunri?' they asked. 'Don't your women have more male children to send to win the bride?' Her husband's clansmen, the party of cousins and uncles who accompanied him, talked readily enough. 'Bheema's father is away. He is a well-known trader and has many places to visit, much buying and selling to do,' his uncle answered them. 'And a number of men from our clan are away too because of the bullock fair. But Bheema's mother did not want to wait. She wanted to have her daughter-in-law brought home without delay, so we decided to come and fetch Bhaunri.' 'And the handsome Bheema? Did he not want his bride too?' one of the women taunted. 'Now that he has seen your Bhaunri, he is sure to want her,' one of the young men in the party replied. The women giggled. They sang ribald songs about Bhaunri's in-laws, about illicit relationships and wild love-makings and children born out of wedlock and raised secretly in straw baskets. This was customary, and the uncle and cousins listened with relish, taunting the women for being too shy. 'Such tame gaali!' they exclaimed. 'In our village the gaali sung by our women can make a stone statue blush.'

THE AFTERNOON WANED and it was time for Bhaunri's departure. From now on, the house she was born and raised in would no longer be her home. The women struck up the doleful bidai song. 'Your carefully nurtured bird, fed on rice and sweet milk, is leaving her father's home,' they sang. 'Now you will not see her nor hear her chirp.' Bhaunri's father clamped the free end of the turban to his eyes and wept. Bhaunri's mother placed one bundle of food and another of Bhaunri's clothes in the cart in which her husband had arrived to fetch her. She held Bhaunri fast to herself; her earring left an imprint on Bhaunri's cheek, her thick silver bracelets dug into Bhaunri's slender back. She tore a strip from her headscarf and held it out to Bhaunri's husband. 'I cover my head with this odhani, son-in-law. It safeguards my honour. I give you a piece of it. Keep my daughter honourably.' Bhaunri's husband nodded, tucked the piece of cloth in his pocket, and climbed into the seat next to the driver's. Bhaunri sat in the back, and the bullocks moved forward lustily. Their hoofmarks and the imprints of the cart's wheels were soon covered by the swirling sand.

Bhaunri pulled her new red headscarf over her face and wrapped herself in the voluminous folds of her skirt. Resting her back against the juddering wooden side of the cart, she fixed her eyes on the free end of the turban falling between her husband's broad shoulders.

3

IT WAS LATE EVENING by the time Bhaunri arrived at her husband's home. The house was large, larger than her father's, and made of bricks and cement. There was a broad, raised platform outside the entranceway on which stood a tall hookah and a pitcher of water. An old cart, painted and decorated with brass and silver ornaments, and with braided colourful silk and gota, leaned against the wall. In a deep niche in the thick wall was an old forge and some rusty looking tools.

Her husband alighted, stretched his arms and called out loudly to his mother. There was no need. She was standing at the threshold peering into the evening gloom. 'Why hasn't the Petromax been lit? This is a house, not a graveyard,' Bheema growled. One of the young cousins hurried inside and soon brought out a brightly lit lantern while Bhaunri's mother-in-law stepped up to the cart. 'Ask the girl to alight. What's she doing in there? Does she think she has come to live in the cart?' Bheema said, taking off his shoes. He struck them together, one against the other, to get rid of the day's dust and entered his father's house. Bhaunri jumped out of the cart nimbly and bent before her mother-in-law. 'May you have many sons and die wearing the red odhani of a suhagan,' her mother-in-law uttered the ritual blessing and, taking her by the arm, ushered her inside. 'Mai, what's the delay in food?' Bheema called as she led Bhaunri towards the house. 'No delay. Everything is ready. All of you get rid of the sand in your mouths and come to eat,' she replied, still holding Bhaunri by the arm.

In the light of the lantern, Bhaunri looked at her mother-in-law. She was small in stature and her complexion was the colour of cooled ghee. Unlike the brief bodice and the wide skirt reaching a little below the calves that Bhaunri wore, her mother-in-law was dressed like a Rajput woman in a full-length lehenga. A blouse reaching down to her waist covered her breasts and back, and the silver edge of her fine, pink odhani was pulled down over her brows. She smiled at Bhaunri. 'Come this way. There's water in the vats. Wash your hands and feet and come to the kitchen.'

Big earthen vats stood in one corner of the large, shadowy courtyard. Bhaunri splashed water on her face and neck, hands and feet, washing off the journey's dust. Her eyes streamed as she thought of her mother cooking at her father's home, slapping thick rotis on to the earthenware griddle, the evening air smelling of browning crusts and hot clay. She wiped her face with her odhani, slipped off her leather mojari by the steps leading into the house, and entered barefoot.

The kitchen was a large room at the front of the house. It had narrow windows and smelt of kerosene. Her mother-in-law was sitting on a low wooden seat in front of the mud chulha. On a kerosene stove under a window, a large aluminium pot with rope-covered handles was bubbling. Bhaunri crouched beside her mother-in-law. 'You roll the rotis, Beendani, I will cook them,' she said and pushed the tray of dough towards her. Bhaunri broke a bit of dough and quickly rolled and flattened it between her palms. She slid it on to the clay griddle glowing with heat. The sound of dogs barking followed by male voices floated in from the courtyard, and Bhaunri's mother-in-law raised her head, her forehead creasing. 'Already here ... I thought they would take some time, smoke a hookah or two...' She went up to the stove and pumped the flame. Bhaunri glanced at her worried face and, taking the iron tongs, began cooking the bread directly in the wood-fire of the chulha. The men trooped in. Bhaunri glanced through the corner of her eye at her husband. He was the tallest, the handsomest among his clansmen, like a prince, she thought.

'Where is the food for my dogs, Mai?' Bheema demanded.

His mother was still bent over the stove, stirring the pot. 'It is almost ready. You begin eating, it will be done in a few minutes.'

'Not ready yet? I'll see how anyone touches a morsel before my dogs are fed.' He kicked a large brass platter across the room. It rebounded against the pot of dal, spilling some on to the mud floor, and hit the wall with a deafening clang. Bhaunri's hand shook. The roti she was cooking slipped from the grip of the iron tongs and fell into fire. 'You dare feed anyone while my dogs are hungry?' her husband spoke through clenched teeth.

'Bheema, your bride is here, you've just brought her home. She is a mere girl,' Bhaunri's mother-in-law said in a quiet voice.

'So? Now I should be scared of a mere girl? Bring your beendani, it is lonely here, that's all I heard from you day and night. You wanted her here, not I. You women have one job and you can't do it on time.'

'Ram, Ram, Bheema,' the uncle spoke up soothingly. 'Don't be angry. Your mother is right, think of your ladi.'

Bheema swung towards him. Foam flecked his lips. 'You keep out of it. Don't try to sound so pious. Just go on fucking your brother's wife. You can fool everyone, but not me.' He turned around and marched out of the kitchen.

Bhaunri's mother-in-law turned the stove off and picked up the potful of hot meat-gruel. 'Serve food to the menfolk, Bhaunri.' She followed Bheema out.

Bhaunri hurriedly retrieved the roti, burnt to a cinder, from the fire and placed a fresh one into it for cooking. The men settled on the floor on one side of the kitchen, leaning their backs against the wall. She served dal and sweet choorma from the pots into brass platters and pushed them one by one towards them, keeping her eyes on the roti cooking in the fire. Her heart beat hard and she strained her ears to catch her husband's voice over the barking of dogs.

'Don't take his anger to heart, Chhori,' the uncle said as he began eating after sprinkling water around his platter. 'Imagine, if he cares so much for his dogs, how much will he care for you? Don't you agree?' He looked around at the young men for support. No one spoke or nodded.

The din of the dogs lessened and Bheema's voice could be heard above it, 'Shera, you beggar, back! Let Bhoori eat. Motherfuckers...'

'Dogs mean the world to us Gadoliyas, Beendani,' the uncle continued after a pause. 'You must have heard the story of the dogs saving our clan when the fort of Chittor fell?' Bhaunri shook her head as she dropped a piping hot roti into his thaal. 'How is it possible that you haven't heard it? Even an infant with milk dripping from its mouth knows this story.' He chewed his mouthful and swallowed it hastily with a gulp of water. 'The story is from the time of the war the Mughal king waged against our Rana of Chittor, our patron. The enemy surrounded the fort, and eventually people did not have enough to eat. When the Rana saw that his people were starving, he decided to fight one final battle. He and his braves donned their saffron robes. We Lohars equipped them with the sharpest swords and strongest lances from our forges and, barricaded inside the fort, awaited the outcome of the battle. Before evening, bad news reached the fort. The Mughals had treacherously defeated the Rajput army, and the Rana had taken to the hills with the remainder of his men. We must go to him, the leaders of our clan decided, for without us who will craft new weapons for them? They began packing the forges and tools, but the enemy broke into the fort before our people were ready. Our leader learnt that the enemy soldiers were looking for us Lohars particularly. They wanted to capture our clan and make us cast weapons for them – our weapons were far superior to the ones their blacksmiths made. Of course, we could never enter the service of the Mughals. We had taken vows of loyalty to our Rana. There seemed no way left for us except to kill the women and children and die fighting. At that moment, our leader's dog spoke.' The young men guffawed. 'You youngsters can laugh, but that dog was a great magician. He said to the leader: I am faithful to you like you are faithful to your king. Take your clan and escape while I, by my magic, transform my pack to take on the appearance of your people and surrender to the soldiers. But hurry, for my magic can hold only for one pahar.'

'Only a couple of hours? The dog wasn't such a big magician after all!' one of the young men said through a mouthful of choorma. Everyone laughed.

'You buffoons, what do you know? To hold the magic for so long requires intense penance. You can't even hold a hammer for ten minutes – or anything else,' the uncle retorted and continued with his story. 'So that's what happened. The pack resumed its original form after one pahar and the Mughals realized they had been tricked by a pack of dogs. In their rage over losing the famous Lohars, they killed the entire pack, down to the last little puppy. Our clan has kept and honoured dogs ever since.'

'I doubt Bheema keeps the dogs for his dead ancestors' vow. It is for hunting that he keeps them. You need dogs to fetch dead birds in thickets and salt-pans,' one of Bheema's cousins remarked.

Bhaunri's mother-in-law returned with the empty pot of dog food. She placed it in a corner and fetched water for everyone. Bhaunri glanced towards the door. There was no sign of Bheema. The din of the dogs had subsided completely.

'Bhavat, I told daughter-in-law not to think much about Bheema's behaviour. That is just his way. There is strength in his body, so every little thing troubles him. Bhai was no different when he was young but look at him now, like an old ox he is majestic but no longer frightening.'

'Dyor-sa, have some more laddoos.' Bhaunri's mother-in-law served several sweets into his platter. She pressed more food on everyone, and by the time the men finished and left the kitchen to chat and smoke their chillum in the courtyard, the night had darkened and Venus was hanging low like a loose jewel in Kalika Mai's earring.

Bhaunri stacked up the utensils in preparation for washing them. Her mother-in-law called, 'Come, Bhaunri, come and eat. It is late. Let those vessels be, you must be hungry. It was a long, dusty journey and you haven't had a sip of water since coming here.'

'And him, Mai? Won't he eat?'

Mai poured ghee over the bajra roti. 'I have served food for both of us in one thaal. You and I are now joined, too. Like you, I had left my mother and father to come to this house,' Bhaunri's mother-in-law spoke softly. Breaking a piece of bajra roti, she fed it to Bhaunri with a lump of jaggery. 'The first mouthful, a sweet mouthful, may your new life be as sweet,' she chanted the familiar formula. Bhaunri's eyes stung and the morsel stuck in her throat. She looked towards the door again. 'Eat, Chhori. He won't eat here tonight. Anger has never filled stomachs and he is not a doddering child. There are plenty of places in the village where he can find food.' She wiped Bhaunri's eyes and cheeks with the end of her fine headscarf. 'Don't worry, Chhori, I will look after you. Don't be afraid of him. I am your mother too, now.'

Bhaunri raised her head and her eyes met Mai's. A half smile appeared around her mouth, her eyes gleamed and she arched her neck. 'I am not afraid of him.'

Mai looked at her in astonishment.

THE NEXT DAY, women from the village came to see the new bride. They shook their heads at the sight of her dark skin and light eyes.

'Such a fair and handsome young man as Bheema, and you found her this one with the complexion of a raincloud? If you had searched properly, you would have easily found him a bride with a moon-like complexion.'

'Yes, and look at her eyes. Just like a cat's. And everyone knows cats feel no maya. They don't love even their own young...'

Bhaunri's mother-in-law wrinkled her brow. 'What are you saying? Don't you have eyes in your faces?' She placed two fingers under Bhaunri's chin and raised her head. 'Look at her, she has skin like velvet and eyes in which stars drown. She is as tall as a doorpost and lovelier than a date palm, more curved than the Ghaggar river herself. I couldn't have wanted a more beautiful daughter-in-law.'

'But we are not talking about you, Bheema ki Ma, you are not the one she is married to! Everyone knows what a rasiya Bheema is. For such a lover of pleasures as him, you needed someone different. This one's so young too, she wouldn't know how to keep him. They are as far apart as the sky and earth. This match won't work. I can draw three lines in the sand and proclaim it today,' an older woman said, shaking her head.

Bhaunri tilted her head and looked at the woman who was speaking. The irises of her deep eyes glowed. 'But the sky and earth have been matched since before time, Kaki-sa. In my village, they say that it is the earth's wishes which cause the sky to fill with desire for her in the month of Saavan.'

The woman raised her eyebrows. 'Bheema's mother, watch out, your daughter-in-law talks like the satbahini myna. I wonder where she learnt to speak like this.'

'I learnt it with the first sip of my mother's milk, Kaki-sa,' Bhaunri smiled.

The women bit their tongues and shook their heads. The consensus in the village was that Bheema's bride spoke out of turn and crossed words with her elders. How she would manage with Bheema's unruly temper in that strange household was anybody's guess, but they would not wager their worst runt against a bull-calf on the chance of Bhaunri being able to stay with her husband for long.

MAI KEPT BHAUNRI close to herself. All day long, Bhaunri followed her, not finding the opportunity to venture farther than the house-door on most days. Neighbours seldom visited them, and Mai did not go out unless it was to buy groceries at the weekly market. Usually, the only people Bhaunri would see besides Mai were the bhishti who fetched water for the household and the boy from the shop who came for Bheema's food in the afternoon.

On days the boy did not show up, Bhaunri wondered what Bheema would eat. 'He sends the boy when he needs food,' Mai answered curtly when she eventually asked. Though she did not ask again, the question troubled Bhaunri as she washed gwar and sangri beans, and spread them to dry in the courtyard, ground gram and pounded millet, learnt to make savouries and sweets from wheat flour.

She sometimes saw her husband in the morning, asleep on a string cot under the mango tree in the courtyard, wrapped in a cotton coverlet. But mostly, she saw him in the evening at dinnertime. As she cooked in the kitchen, Bhaunri's whole being was concentrated in her ears, to pick out the sounds signalling Bheema's return. He often brought his dogs along from where he kennelled them near the fields at the outskirts of the village. He fed them first and then ate himself. Bhaunri cooked hot rotis for him and Mai sat beside him, refilling his plate while he ate in silence. When he finished and rose to leave, Bhaunri's eyes followed him to the door. Often, she heard him leave the house and call to his dogs. He never looked at or spoke to her.

At night, she slept beside her mother-in-law in the tiny room near the storehouse that smelt of woodsmoke and ghee and camphor.

4

SLOWLY, DESPITE MAI'S EFFORTS to keep her indoors, Bhaunri went out into the village. On one occasion when the curd set loosely and needed careful churning, a task that Mai could not leave to Bhaunri, and fine-ground wheat flour was needed for making sweets, Bhaunri offered to take the grain to the mill.

'Let it be, Beendani, we will make do with what we can grind at home,' Mai said.

'But we can never grind as fine as the mill with our chakki, Mai,' Bhaunri said and picked up the sack.

'Then we will make the sweet another day. It is hot outside and you don't know where to go...'

'I know where the flour mill is. You keep me tied to your odhani's end, Mai. In my village, I grazed the goats and fetched water from the baoli every day,' Bhaunri said, smiling. Mai had to reluctantly permit her to go.

THE MILLER TOOK the grain and poured it into the grinder. His talkative daughter came out of the house and, taking Bhaunri by the hand, led her to the corner where empty sacks were stacked. They sat on the coarse mound of bags surrounded by the fresh smell and fine dust of new flour.

'Why did you not come for Vat Pooja last week?' the miller's daughter asked.

'Mai said we should pray at the tree outside our door.'

'She used to join the rest of us in the past. Now she stays at home always and keeps you close to her like her shadow. You go nowhere, not to the baoli or the temple.'

'It's just that we have so much to do at home. Two of the cows have calved, and we have raw mango and ker pickles to prepare before the fruit becomes very dry.'

'So why won't she call us to help, or pay one of the Kaharans? Your father-in-law has plenty of money.'

'He is not home, my father-in-law...'

'Oh, he is always roaming now. It is a mercy he is not home. Such tantrums he used to throw, such rage he would fly into. And the fights your Bheema and he used to have, like two wild boars. Once, your father-in-law beat up your mother-in-law so badly the Panch had to intervene. We had to feed her roti softened in milk like a toothless babe for days, and apply turmeric and old ghee on her bruises.'

'But why did he beat her?'

'Why do men beat their lugais? Because there is another one somewhere.'

'You mean he has married another woman?'

'No, no, why would he do that? Why plant a tree if you can have fruit from another's?'

'That can't be true. Why would Mai let him?'

The miller's daughter laughed. 'Which world have you come from? Since when does a man need his wife's permission to do anything? Does Bheema ask you? He is no different. Like father, like son.'

Bhaunri's breath swelled. She picked up the sack of flour, paid the miller and walked back home.

Mai looked at her moist eyes. 'What happened, Chhori? You fell?'

Bhaunri shook her head. 'The miller's daughter, she said Bheema has another woman. Is it true, Mai?'

'She talks nonsense. When one is idle, one gossips, and that girl never lifts a finger to work, only wags her tongue,' Mai said. 'Don't lend your ear to worthless talk, daughter. It brings unease. Come, the flour won't roast itself. This evening we will make sweets. I have made plenty of butter.' Bhaunri followed her into the kitchen.

That evening she cast sidelong looks at her husband. He ate in silence, chewing his food thoroughly, his mouth wet and shiny with buttermilk, his eyes abstracted. To Bhaunri, he seemed as handsome as the sun god, and as remote.

MAI'S MOANS WOKE Bhaunri up. Usually Mai was up before sunrise to tend to the cows but today she was still in bed. Bhaunri felt her forehead with the back of her hand. It was hot and clammy with a sticky sweat. Bhaunri fetched oil and old bits of cloth. She rubbed Mai's forehead, hands and feet with the oil, and tied cloth over her aching joints.

'Chhori, ask the bhishti to wait when he comes. I have some work for him. There is lapsi in the pot. Give it to your husband for his breakfast. I will try to get up in some time...'

Bhaunri looked at her blotched face and heavy eyes. 'Don't worry, Mai, you rest. I will prepare some kadha for you.'

'There is the housework...'

'I can manage it all, Mai. I used to work on the forge and do housework in my father's home.'

Later in the morning, the bhishti came to fill the big earthen vats with water from his goatskin.

'Could you wait?' Bhaunri asked. 'Mai is unwell and she has some work for you.'

'Oh ho, your mother-in-law is not well? Of course, I will stay. She will want me to feed the mad one and deliver Bheema's lunch.'

'Mad one? Whom do you mean?'

'Your jeth, Bheema's elder brother, of course.'

Bhaunri stared. 'His elder brother? Where is he?'

'Where is he?' the bhishti raised his eyebrows. 'Where would he be, the bawla? He lives in the little room in the cowshed. You have been here for months now. Don't you know? It is only a woman like your mother-in-law who could do the penance of looking after him. Anyone else would have turned him out on the street. He can't do anything for himself. She bathes him and feeds him like a baby every day. And she is the only one who can calm him down when he gets angry. No one dares to go near him then. He can stun a full-grown bullock with a single blow and rip the iron hinges of the door out. I have seen him do it myself. Bring your pots and let me fill them for you, I have some water left in my mashak.'

Bhaunri brought the earthen pots from the kitchen. The bhishti bent at the waist and sent a stream of water into them from the goatskin he carried slung across his body. He helped her lift the pots to carry indoors, balanced on the ornamented cloth-ring her mother had made for her. 'Don't wait. I can manage. You go on your rounds,' she said to him.

The pot of lentils on the chulha was bubbling. She placed the water pots in a corner and began kneading dough. Her thoughts returned to what the bhishti had told her. She had always marvelled at Mai's devotion to the cows and buffaloes. First thing in the morning, Mai disappeared into the cowshed. She always cleaned the shed and milked the cows by herself. 'Mai, back at home I looked after cows too. Let me help you,' Bhaunri had said once or twice, but Mai had just smiled and shaken her head. 'The colour of bridal mehendi has not long left your palms. I don't want them to smell of cow dung so soon.' At mealtimes, Mai filled a large platter with food and disappeared into the shed. Bhaunri had assumed the food was for the cows, the first morsels set aside for them to ensure plenty in the household. She didn't know that, all this time, there was a mad brother-in-law concealed in the cowshed.

When the food was ready, she set aside a pile of thick bread smeared with ghee in a brass platter and a big bowl full of dal. Then, filling a brass tumbler with the medicinal drink she had made with coriander seeds, carom and dried roots, she carried it to Mai's room. Mai's eyes were closed, a strip of cloth tied around her forehead, her face creased with pain.

'Mai, I have brought you some kadha.' Bhaunri placed the tumbler on the floor and helped Mai into a sitting position. 'Drink it, the fever will break.'

Mai took a few sips. 'Beendani, I feel bad putting all the household work on your shoulders. You are still a child.'

'Don't worry, Mai, I can manage.'

Mai drank the kadha and placed her hand on Bhaunri's head in blessing. 'You are a daughter, not a daughter-in-law. May God shower all his blessings on you.' She lay down again and closed her eyes.

Bhaunri picked up the empty tumbler. 'Food's ready. I will take Jeth-ji his lunch now.'

Mai's eyes flew open. She looked at Bhaunri as she squatted beside her pallet. 'Chhori,' she began, but her throat choked.

'Don't worry, Mai. I will do everything,' Bhaunri repeated and rose. 'I have kept Bheema's food ready in case he sends someone from the shop.' She turned to go.

'Daughter-in-law, call me if there is a problem with Mangla, your jeth,' Mai said softly.

'There won't be.'

Bhaunri balanced the platter of food on the flat of her palm, tucked the pitcher of water under one arm and stepped into the cowshed. In all the months she had been in her husband's home, Bhaunri had never entered the cowshed. She had caught glimpses of it from the courtyard as she went about her tasks. It was a long room that ran along the side of the house. Unlike the cattle shed at her father's house which was open on two sides, this one was enclosed and its thatched roof was high. There was a small room with a high, barred window at the far end. As she cautiously unlatched the door, Bhaunri felt a little giddy. It was dim inside the room. She narrowed her eyes and saw a man sitting cross-legged on a string cot. Head raised, eyes fixed on the door, he sat motionless. Bhaunri caught her breath. Despite the unkempt hair and beard, there was no mistaking the resemblance to Bheema. She stepped forward and her foot knocked over the metal pitcher beside the cot. The man did not blink.

'Jeth-ji, I have brought your food.' Bhaunri placed the platter before him. Her husband's brother stared at her in silence. Then he picked up a roti and began eating it in big mouthfuls, never taking his eyes off her. She filled the pitcher with water and watched as he ate. 'Eat the roti with dal,' she said softly. Mangla's eyes, except for a certain heaviness, were just like Bheema's. Bhaunri broke a morsel, crumbled onion and green chilli in it, dipped it in the bowl of lentils, and held it towards him. He slowly extended his hand and took the mouthful, quickly stuffing it into in his mouth. Bhaunri squatted by the cot and fed him. When he finished, he drank water directly from the pitcher and burped loudly. Bhaunri collected the thali and lota and stepped out, closing the door behind her. At the threshold of the cowshed, she turned. She could see Mangla's shaggy head as he stood peeping at her through the narrow window.

IN THE EVENING, Bheema returned. He entered the kitchen. Bhaunri was adjusting the fire in the mud oven, her back towards the door. She heard him enter and said over her shoulder, 'Mai is unwell, she has fever. The food for your dogs is ready.'

He stood in silence, watching her as she finished arranging wood in the chulha and rose. Her back was bare save for the strings which held her kanchali in place, and the folds of her ghaghra flared and swayed over her hips as she stepped to the window where the pot of dog food stood cooling.

'I have prepared this for the first time,' she said, holding the pot out to Bheema. 'I have cooked it with more care than a mother cooks her baby's gruel, but please forgive me if there is any mistake.' Her eyes, the colour of winter sunlight, rested on his. The pale chooda on her arms clanged as she handed him the pot. He stared at her bold eyes, shook his head slightly and left the kitchen.

Bhaunri returned to her place before the chulha and began freshening the dough with drops of water. She could still feel Bheema's startled gaze, as if it were touching her bare skin. Something welled up inside her with a painful intensity. She wanted to see herself reflected in those eyes again. She pressed her knees to her chest and drew a long breath.

Bheema returned after feeding the dogs. He had washed his hands and feet in the courtyard, and his wet footprints glistened on the clean mud floor. He sat in the far corner and ate in silence as usual. Bhaunri stole glances at him, her eyes lingered on his bowed head, his shoulders, his broad chest, the folds of the dhoti pulled tight across his legs and loins.

When he finished, she went to Mai's room and cajoled her into eating a few bites. Afterwards, she filled a platter with food for her brother-in-law. Bheema saw her crossing the courtyard from where he sat at the threshold, smoking a chillum. 'Here,' he called out to her. 'Where are you going?'

'Taking your brother his dinner.'

Bheema crossed the courtyard in a couple of strides and took the platter from her. 'You go eat yourself, I'll feed him.' He turned and disappeared inside the cowshed.

Bhaunri ate, and washed and tidied the kitchen. Then she filled the brass pitcher with water, put a lump of jaggery in a small bowl, and carried both out to the courtyard. Bheema was nowhere in sight. She placed the pitcher near his string cot, covering it with the bowl. Picking up the rolled bedding and the coarse cotton sheet, she shook them out before spreading them on the cot. When Bheema returned, he saw her standing in the shade of the mango tree which was just beginning to bear sprigs of small, pale flowers.

At the sound of his footsteps, Bhaunri turned and watched him approach. Bheema bent and picked up the lota. He put the piece of jaggery in his mouth and drank the water. He had taken off his shirt, and his wrestler's body glowed pale in the blue shade of the tree. Bhaunri felt there was a large magnet right at the centre of Bheema's chest which drew her like a bit of iron. She stretched her hand and touched the angle where the column of his neck joined his broad shoulder, and let her fingers trail on to his chest. Bheema set the lota down.

'Chhori...' He held her wrist.

'My name is Bhaunri,' she said.

'Beendani...' Mai called from inside the house. 'Daughter-in-law...'

Bheema dropped her hand. Bhaunri stepped away and walked towards the house with slow steps.

BHAUNRI LOOKED FORWARD to the mornings now. Every morning Bheema helped her clean the cowshed and milk the cows. She liked working side by side with him. Their hands brushed against each other, their bodies touched, and Bheema's veiled eyes rested longer and longer on her. In the evenings, he returned home earlier and sat in the courtyard playing with his dogs or plaiting rope or smoking his chillum. Bhaunri caught glimpses of him as she moved about the house and courtyard. The songs her mother had sung came back to her, songs about a peacock enamoured of the clouds, calling to them, of young women fetching water from the baoli, of a lonely camel in the boundless desert. Unconsciously, she sang snatches of them, her eyes seeking Bheema as she went about her chores.

Mai watched Bhaunri with worried eyes. She called her as soon as the evening meal was over and Bhaunri sat by her side, rubbing her temples with mustard oil, pressing her feet, massaging her back until she dropped to sleep.

ONE NIGHT, BHAUNRI went to the house-door to toss the kitchen sweepings for birds to eat in the morning. Bheema was squatting at the threshold, smoking. As she turned back, he held her by the end of her odhani.

'I got this for you. From the town.' He took her hand and placed a small vial of perfume in her palm. Bhaunri looked at him in the dark doorway, her body tingling, and tucked the little bottle into her kanchali.

The next day, after her bath, Bhaunri dabbed the perfume on her body and rubbed some into the end of her odhani. Mai looked at her sharply as she brought her lunch.

'I can smell attar, rose attar.'

'He gave me some last night,' Bhaunri replied, her mouth curved in a smile, her eyes lit up like diyas.

That evening, Mai got up and came to the kitchen. She wouldn't listen to Bhaunri's protests and sat beside the chulha breathing laboriously, her back resting against the wall. 'A woman's place is in the rasoda, that's where she ought to live and die,' she said and peeled onions with slow fingers.

AFTER MAI RECOVERED completely, the old routine resumed, but Bhaunri knew something had changed. She could feel Bheema's eyes following her. The silence, piled up like sand between them, blew away. He spoke to her even if it was just to chide her for not cooking the roti crisper. He helped her lift the pots full of water, held the young, frisky cow when Bhaunri milked her, and brought sweets home when he saw Bhaunri eating a lump of brown, fragrant khand.

One afternoon, Mai went to the weekly market leaving Bhaunri home as usual. Bhaunri decided to wash her hair. She closed the street-door. There was no latch on the inside so she placed a large pan against it. If a neighbour decided to visit or Mai returned earlier than expected, the clatter of the falling pan would warn her. She boiled some shikakai beans with soap-nut and undid the numerous plaits Mai had arranged her hair in. She filled a bucket with water and dragged Bheema's string cot to a corner of the courtyard. She stood it on its end and, behind this makeshift screen, quickly undressed. After washing her hair, she rubbed her body with a mixture of rough-ground millet flour and milk until her limbs gleamed, and scrubbed her feet with a bit of stone. As she poured cold water over her body heated by the sun, the pan clattered to the ground and the street-door swung open. It was Bheema.

Astonished, Bhaunri pulled down the rough cotton towel and wrapped it around her. 'Mai has gone to the haat,' she said from the other side of the cot, her eyes on Bheema's.

He came forward and pushed the cot away with his foot. Bhaunri rose. The thin cotton cloth stuck to her wet body, her bare shoulders were beaded with water. Her dripping hair trailed in dark streaks down her back. Bheema stood arrested.

'Ladi,' he said hoarsely, 'come here.' Bhaunri swayed towards him like a bajra stalk in the wind. She reached out and touched his face, his ears, the muscles on his neck. Bheema breathed deeply and pulled her to him by the waist.

A wild cry sounded from the back of the house, followed by the mooing of cows and the clatter of their hooves. Bheema let go of her. 'Mangla has managed to get out. Go inside, girl.' He sprinted towards the cowshed. Bhaunri snatched up her clothes and went indoors.

IN THE EVENING, when Bheema came home, Bhaunri brought water and coals for his chillum. He plucked the coals and arranged them carefully in the clay pipe. She stood watching him.

'What's the matter?' he asked gruffly.

She smiled and shook her head. 'Nothing.'

Their eyes locked, and Bhaunri knew that their hearts had met finally, Bheema's and hers.

5

JUST BEFORE THE BLOSSOMS on the mango tree began dropping like tiny, pale butterflies, Bhaunri's father-in-law returned. The village kids had seen him striding along the path which passed through the fields and hurried over to inform Bhaunri's mother-in-law. It was early evening, and Bhaunri and her mother-in-law were both in the courtyard, resting before beginning preparations for the evening meal. Bhaunri was massaging Mai's hair with warm oil.

'Kaki, Kako-sa is coming. He has a big bag slung over his shoulder,' they sang out. 'His eyes are red, his feet are dustier than ours.'

On hearing the children's chants, Mai opened her eyes. Her face tightened and she sighed. 'Bhaunri, give the children some gudia shakkar,' she said and rose, 'then hurry up and come along. We need to prepare dinner.' At the entrance of the house, she stopped. 'Put the remaining oil in your hair and braid it carefully. Your father-in-law does not like loose or messy hair.' Bhaunri nodded.

As she oiled and braided her hair, Bhaunri sighed too. She had now been in her husband's home for over six months. The shadow of the unseen father-in-law had hovered over the household during that time. One evening, Bhaunri had asked about him as she and her mother-in-law sifted grain in the courtyard. 'When will father-in-law return? Will he be back before Shravan begins, Mai?' Shravan, the month of rains, was full of festivals. Everyone came home for Shravan, lovers met, peacocks danced, the earth revived – even the tired earth of the Thar desert. Instead of Mai, Bheema had answered. He had returned early and was sitting on the threshold, plaiting rope. Rearing his head like an angry bull he had said, 'What has that to do with you, woman? The longer he stays away, the better for this household.'

Besides the miller's daughter, Bhaunri had heard from others about her father-in-law's wayward ways too. People spoke about his drinking, his blind anger, his strength and craftiness. 'He has a great temper, your father-in-law,' the bhishti had told her once, 'anger like a real Rana.' He had widened his eyes. 'He once picked up a man and threw him into the nearby dam, he is that strong.' 'Did the man die?' Bhaunri asked. 'No, no, your father-in-law jumped after him and saved him. If that man had died, it would have meant police and courts and money down the drain. He is no fool, your father-in-law,' the bhishti had laughed.

THERE HAD ALSO been the incident when the Mukhbancha Bhat had come around to sing the genealogies of village folk. Bhaunri and her mother-in-law had prepared a meal for the Bhat, and sweets and savouries for the listeners. 'Our family is the most prosperous in this village,' Mai had explained, 'so we have always discharged the duties of a patron towards the Bhats.' She had set aside money in silver coins for their fee. 'They preserve the name and tales of our ancestors. All this is nothing, mere mud compared to the gold of the memories they keep safe in their songs,' she had said.

Bhaunri understood. These oral genealogists used to pass through her village too, and sing songs about the origin of various clans, telling and retelling fantastical tales of blacksmiths endowed with remarkable abilities. She particularly remembered the story of the first of her father's ancestors, a strapping, handsome Lohar, who had won for his king a crucial battle. The enemy army had been stronger, but the Lohar had come up with a plan. He crafted a sickle, shining and perfectly shaped like the curved moon, and hung it high on a date palm after the real moon had set. The timekeeper for the enemy army was fooled by the sickle-moon. He let his soldiers sleep, thinking the moon was high in the sky and it was still midnight. The Lohar's patron king took advantage of the enemy's tardiness and his armies advanced. By the time the enemy king realized the trick, it was too late. His camp was overwhelmed and he himself perished fighting. The enemy king's queen cursed the Lohar just before entering the fire with her dead husband's body, 'You used the moon to trick my husband. Like the moon, your clan will wax and wane. Just when your clan reaches the peak of prosperity, their decline will begin, misfortunes will beset you. Ever so often, your offspring will lose everything and roam the desert searching for sustenance.' 'And it is true,' her father would say after every recital of the familiar tale, 'in my own family, my grandfather was cheated of everything, even his cart and bullocks were taken when he was returning to the family camp after earning a fortune at a fair.' Bheema had overheard her reciting parts of the story to Mai, and when she went to collect his clothes for washing, he had pinched her waist. 'Deceiver's daughter! I did not know your ancestors were so crafty.' 'Now you do,' Bhaunri had flashed him a glance, 'so beware.'

The Bhat had set up his instruments on the platform outside the house. Before beginning the performance, he had asked, 'Where is the jajman with whose genealogy we will commence our recital?'

'He is away,' Mai answered, setting a large earthen lamp filled with oil by his side.

'Even if he were in the village, Bhat Maharaj, you'd need to tell a different story if you wanted him to come,' one of the women said archly.

'And you'd need to be a Nattin or a Kanjar girl to whisper the story into his hairy ear. Though he is more likely to tell that sort of a story to a girl than hear it,' another commented.

'Who? Him or his son,' a third young woman added.

Everyone laughed. Mai turned fiercely at them. 'It is a solemn occasion. These Bhats are gunis. Can't you girls keep sullied thoughts out of your heads even for a few hours?'

There was a momentary silence. The men and women shook their heads. 'Money has gone to her head. Hearing the truth hurts worse than a scorpion's sting,' they whispered to each other. Bhaunri blinked hard. Her eyes pricked as if they were filled with sand. She waited impatiently for the performance to end.

Mai was busy putting away unused provisions after the performance when Bhaunri went up to her. 'What did they mean, Mai?'

'Who?' Mai turned away to put the canister of ghee in a niche high in the wall of the storehouse.

'The women, when they were speaking about the Kanjar girls.' There were girls belonging to the Kanjar tribe in a settlement outside Bhaunri's father's village. She knew they practised prostitution.

'Don't bother your head about what the women said, Chhori. As there are mouths, so there is chatter. The greater the jealousy, the worse the gossip.'

'But the things they said about father-in-law and Bheema...'

'Daughter, your father-in-law is a man. Whatever he does, it becomes him.'

'But you are his dhani. He must please you, or else why would your heart cleave to him?'

Mai glanced at her and sighed. 'Come, eat,' she said.

'BHAUNRI...' MAI CALLED, and Bhaunri hurried indoors. She felt a certainty that everything would change, now that her father-in-law was home.

Mai had lit the chulha and was filling the pot with scraps of meat and pieces of bones, when Bhaunri entered the kitchen. 'Here, take care of the food for the dogs. And slice these mateeri.' She pointed to a basket full of small, green, striped fruit. 'We will also cook kheepoli. Your father-in-law is fond of those beans,' she said and stepped out of the kitchen.

Bhaunri quickly sliced the vegetables and kneaded the dough. Her mother-in-law returned carrying a freshly slaughtered chicken. She set it on a platter and began plucking it. 'I asked the neighbours to let us have one for today. Tomorrow, I must get a few hens. We'll need them while your father-in-law is here.'

Bheema loved goat meat and often brought it home when he returned in the evening, or brought back meat of nilgai and wild fowl when he went on a hunt. Bhaunri's mother-in-law cooked it with garlic and freshly ground spices. 'Father-in-law does not like laal maans, Mai?' Bhaunri asked.

Mai glanced at her. 'Your father-in-law likes chicken. Pay attention, I will show you how to cook it. And roast some old rice, once the dog food is done.' She began slicing onions.

Bheema returned after sundown. He sniffed at the sweet and savoury smells in the kitchen. The corners of his eyes tightened and his forehead creased. He picked up the pot of dog food and, walking out, spoke over his shoulder, 'You women are crazy. You are cooking a king's feast for that good for nothing, while he is sitting at the theka, drinking himself silly. By the time he is done and comes home, he won't know whether he is eating food or shoe-leather.' He stalked out.

Bhaunri's mother-in-law sighed deeply and removed the meat from the fire. 'This is ready, but if he is drinking, he won't be back soon. Make some rotis for Bheema, he is hungry.'

Bhaunri fanned the flames in the chulha and began rolling the dough.

IT WAS LATE by the time Bhaunri's father-in-law returned to the home he had left many months ago. Everyone had eaten, and Bhaunri was tidying the kitchen. Bheema had left to put his dogs in their kennel near the fields. Mai raised her head at the sound of the street-door. Heavy footsteps sounded in the courtyard.

'Woman, where are you?' The voice was deep and dry-edged like a desert well.

Bhaunri saw a shudder, like a ripple in the sand, pass through Mai's body. 'See if the food is hot ... He is here,' she said quietly to Bhaunri.

Bhaunri took out the bread she had buried among the hot ashes of the chulha and served it along with the meat on a platter made of dry leaves set out by her mother-in-law.

'Wife, I am home.' Bhaunri's father-in-law stood in the doorway. He was a big man, taller than both his sons, and large-boned. His tanned skin was almost as dark as Bhaunri's, and he had a tight little potbelly. He tottered on his large feet and grabbed hold of the doorpost for support. He peered at Bhaunri. 'Who is this?'

Mai rose. She kept her eyes lowered. 'Will you wash your hands and feet before eating?' she asked, addressing him formally.

'Forget about my hands and feet, Lugai. Do lions wash? Who is this girl?'

'She is your daughter-in-law. Bheema's wife. He brought her home while you were away.'

'Daughter-in-law!' he exclaimed. 'She has grown. When I saw her, she was a snivelling girl, and now she is beautiful like Moomal. Girl, when did you get breasts round like a kumhar's pot and a waist the width of my hand? If I had known, I would not have matched you with Bheema.'

Mai moved between her husband and Bhaunri, screening her. 'Don't worry, Bhaunri, don't be afraid. Your father-in-law is joking.'

'Joking? Joking? Who is joking? Daughter-in-law or not, remove this young woman from in front of me. I am drunk and won't be answerable for what I do.' He lurched into the kitchen.

Bhaunri rose and, arching her neck, turned her steady eyes on to her father-in-law. She picked up the pitcher of water. 'I will take this to Bheema now, Mai. My work here is done.'

'Bheema, Bheema,' jeered her father-in-law as she stepped out of the kitchen. 'What can little Bheema do? Nothing. He can only flex his muscles and push the boys in his akhada around.'

Bheema was not in the courtyard. Bhaunri stood for a moment in the shade of the mango tree. She did not wish to return indoors. The night air was fresh and fragrant with late blossoms, and clouds drifted in the luminescent sky. Songs imploring the rains to fall plentifully resounded in the village.

At last, reluctantly, she returned to the house. There was no one in the kitchen. She could hear her mother-in-law moving around the house. Bhaunri warmed the milk and set the curd, swept the ashes and sprinkled a pinch of dry dough and droplets of water on the clay griddle. She sat on her haunches for a few moments, undecided as to what to do next. Then she stepped out of the kitchen and went to Mai's room.

Her father-in-law was sitting on the cot. The room smelt of a mixture of local brew, sweat and leather. 'What do you want, my daughter-in-law?' he asked heavily. 'Weren't you going to your Bheema? What are you doing here?'

Bhaunri looked at her mother-in-law bent in a corner, fiddling with the wick of the lantern. 'I sleep here.'

'What?' Her father-in-law turned to his wife, 'You keep her tied to your ghaghra's string? You want her to be like you, whimpering if her man comes near her?' He rose and came to the door. He towered over Bhaunri, his head touching the plinth. 'Don't stand here, Chhori. Go. Go to your man and, if he has anything left in him, he will till you like a fecund field.' Bhaunri looked at her mother-in-law who stood white-faced and still in the corner. 'Don't stand there looking at her. She hasn't been doing you a favour, making you sleep here night after night, saving you from your husband – just as she wishes someone would save her from hers.'

Bhaunri turned her pale, cold eyes on him. 'I don't need saving from my husband.'

Her father-in-law laughed. 'I believe you. You are like a wild cat. Go away now. I need my wife.' He closed the door with a bang.

Bhaunri stood looking at the closed door for a few moments. Slowly, she turned and walked towards the courtyard.

THE NIGHT WAS dark. A thin moon had risen, but the mango tree was like an impenetrable fort of darkness. Bhaunri caught the gleam of the metal pitcher in the layered shadows under it. Everything else was indistinguishable.

She crossed the courtyard. Her ankle bracelets clanged against each other, the little bells on her waistband tinkled. On the cot under the tree, Bheema lay flat on his back, his arm across his eyes. Bhaunri stood listening to her husband's breathing for a moment then, stepping closer, she sat at the foot of the cot. The pit of her stomach contracted, warmth exuded like waves from her body. Bheema moved his arm and gazed at Bhaunri.

'I can't sleep in Mai's kothari tonight,' she said.

Wordlessly, Bheema reached out an arm and pulled her to himself. One end of Bhaunri's odhani caught on the rough-hewn wooden post of the cot. She pulled out the other end tucked into her waistband, releasing the scarf and allowing it to flutter down beside the cot. Bheema's arms circled her, pressing her against himself. Bhaunri felt lightheaded, blood beat in unfamiliar places in her body. It was like the time she and other children had taken swigs of daaru at a wedding while their parents were busy elsewhere. Everyone else had been sick, but she had felt light, floating like a chain of jasmine flowers.

She touched Bheema's chest, his shoulders. 'You are like iron,' she whispered.

'I am a Lohar, I am made of iron.' He tightened his grip around her. 'Haven't you heard the story of Vishwakarma?' Bhaunri shook her head. 'You are ignorant. Vishwakarma was the blacksmith of the gods. Once, in an idle moment, he crafted some figures out of the iron he made divine weapons with. His puppets were so beautiful that Brahma became enamoured of them and brought them to life. That's how we Lohars came into existence.' He caressed Bhaunri's face roughly. 'But you are only half a blacksmith, you are not made of iron.'

'What am I made of then?'

'I want to find out too.' His hand slipped down Bhaunri's neck, her swelling breasts, down to her stomach where the muscles were taut. He touched the fleshy mound in which her deep navel was set and slid his fingers inside her skirt. Bhaunri trembled and let out a long sigh. 'You are an ear of millet, Chhori, fragrant and full,' Bheema whispered. 'You are my ear of millet to reap...'

Bhaunri knew the song. It was sung during the night-long celebration when a bride first comes to her groom's house. Relatives and village folk gathered at night to sing songs of love and desire while the bride and groom spent their first night together.

'We did not have our ratijaga,' Bhaunri said.

'Tonight is our ratijaga, my golden girl,' Bheema hummed. 'Tonight I am the peacock and you are the rain.'

He tugged at the strings of her kanchali, slipped off her ghaghra. Breathing deeply, he straddled her. Bhaunri put her strong arms around her husband's perfect body, a body so beautiful, she had to grit her teeth and close her eyes to bear it. There, under the setting moon and the rustling blue shade of the mango tree, Bhaunri and her husband mated.

Afterwards, as they lay side by side in silence under the same cotton coverlet, Bhaunri curled herself around her Bheema. Her head on his chest, she heard the thunder in his blood. Filled with a deep satisfaction, she fell into dreamless sleep.

SHE WOKE JUST after the morning star had set and the sky was brightening with the first light of dawn. Her head had slipped off Bheema's chest. She lay looking at him in the oncoming light. Bheema was sleeping on his back, his eyes, his face, his whole body seemed closed upon itself, closed away from her. Her heart beat hard and she tried to swallow the unknown fears filling her throat. Tears fell from her eyes.

Bhaunri entered the cowshed to help her mother-in-law with the morning milking, her cheeks still damp with tears. Mai was crouched beside the great black cow, her head against its flank, her fingers moving slowly, blindly. On hearing Bhaunri's footsteps she raised her head. Her eyes were dull, the rims red. She looked at Bhaunri's swollen eyes, her cautious movements, and her mouth curved downwards.

'Chhori, are you all right? My poor girl...' her lips trembled. 'It is beastly but there is no recourse, you have to endure it. A she-camel bears the burden of her mate's desire ... At least you had respite for a few months...'

'Mai, I am all right, there's nothing wrong.'

Bhaunri squatted close to her mother-in-law. The cows and buffaloes shuffled restlessly, their udders heavy, waiting for their turn. Usually, the air in the cowshed smelt of bovine bodies, cow dung, fresh feed and milk. Today it seemed to have a different aroma.

'Really, Mai, I am fine.' Mai continued to look at her and Bhaunri smiled. 'Mai, my heart cleaves to him, I feel I can cross the desert barefoot for him.'

Mai's eyes clouded. 'Chhori, do not talk like this ... It is better for the body to endure than for the heart to be snared. It only brings more suffering.'

Bhaunri only half heard her mother-in-law. Her thoughts were on her husband and, unknowingly, involuntarily, she smiled.

'Woman, where are you? Where is my daatun?' Bhaunri's father-in-law called and Mai rose.

'I will milk the cows, Mai. You go,' Bhaunri said. She hoped Bheema would look into the cowshed before leaving for his shop.

6

THE ARRIVAL OF HER father-in-law changed the household's routine completely. Though he'd be late returning home, Bheema stopped spending nights away. He seldom brought his pack of dogs with him to be fed. 'I feed them in the kennel. There is too much to do here with the old demon back,' he said to Bhaunri, throwing a malevolent look towards the house-steps where his father sat smoking his hookah.

He was right about there being much to do. Even though there was only one addition to the household, Mai and Bhaunri's work seemed to have increased manifold. Mai was constantly needed to do something or the other for her husband. His clothes needed mending, his moustache needed trimming, and his hookah needed freshening ever so often. She had to wash and starch his three-coloured turban to the correct degree of stiffness, and cook him a porridge of broken wheat and jaggery every morning. Mai attended to his needs in silence. Most mornings, her eyes were red and puffy, her face pale and tense, as she went about her chores. She only relaxed when her husband left the house. He spent most mornings sitting on the platform outside the house or in the chaupal chatting with people. He had stories to tell from his travels and was always generous with his tobacco and bidis. Though he was no longer a panch, his family having given up iron work customary to the clan, his success in trading, his knowledge of the ways of the world, and the money he lent occasionally to his clansmen, all combined to ensure he never lacked company.

Bhaunri did the morning milking by herself and cleaned the house. She did not mind the extra work, or the constant demands from her father-in-law to cook elaborate dishes – sweet yellow rice one day, choorma the next – to oil his shoes, polish his cart, wash his dhoti with fragrant soap. She did not mind because there was Bheema. Every night after finishing the household chores, she went to him. Every night she lay with her head on his chest, his arms around her, his loins pressed against her. Every night her certainty that their hearts had mated, that they were as one, was renewed. She slept listening to his breath and woke in the warm aura of his body. She gave him his breakfast of buttermilk and bread or porridge or millet gruel in the kitchen, and watched over him in the evening as he ate his meal. She was content.

CLOUDS WERE FLOCKING in the sky, slowly building a promising bank in the west. It was early afternoon. Bhaunri was in the front of the house, sifting lentils for stones and straw. Mai was in the back, feeding the colony of newly-acquired hens. Bhaunri's father-in-law entered through the street-door. He called out to Mai. Bhaunri set down the tray of lentils and came out into the courtyard.

'Mai is in the backyard. Do you need something?'

'Yes, I do,' her father-in-law answered, fixing his bloodshot eyes on her, 'and though you are my son's wife, if you were generous, you could give it to me too.'

Bhaunri frowned. 'I will fetch you buttermilk.'

'Why? I don't need buttermilk. It is not that kind of thirst,' he leered.

Bhaunri raised her head. 'Half my blood is of a murderous clan of Gujjars, my sasura,' she said, looking directly at him with her pale eyes. 'I can slit a man's throat with a sickle just as easily as I slaughter chicken.'

'I thought you were a mere girl but you are quite a woman, daughter-in-law. I wish I were twenty years younger. There was no one like me in the surrounding villages then. Your husband doesn't compare with me. He is like a nameless bush next to the desert palm I was in my youth.' He flexed his arms. 'I can still crush two of him easily.'

'I will tell him. You can sort it out with him yourself.'

Her father-in-law laughed appreciatively. 'Is there another one like you back at your father's home? Is your mother like you too? By the shrine of my ancestors, I will knock on her thatch one of these nights.'

'She rears snakes in her thatch, father-in-law. And though my father can split heads with one stroke of his iron mallet, she doesn't need him to protect her. She is the one who taught me to slit throats.'

Mai entered the courtyard carrying cowpats in an iron pan. She looked at her husband and daughter-in law facing each other. 'What happened? Do you need anything?'

'Nothing that I can get from you, wife, nothing that you can give me. Your daughter-in-law has spoilt my taste. She is a real woman. I bet our son has an adventurous time in bed. Come, pour water on me. I need a bath. I am steaming from the heat.' He turned and, looking at Bhaunri over his shoulder, added, 'You can watch, my daughter-in-law, and see what a real man looks like.'

Bhaunri took the iron pan from Mai's hands. 'I will set out these cowpats for drying. Lunch will be ready soon.'

Mai followed her husband, her head bowed. In his wake, she looked frailer and smaller than usual. Bhaunri's heart welled up. She knew that this was the marriage of sin her mother had warned her about.

After her father-in-law had eaten and lunch was sent for Bheema, Bhaunri served food for her mother-in-law and herself in the same platter. She poured ghee on Mai's roti and sprinkled sugar liberally over it.

Mai smiled. 'You are feeding me sweet bread, my daughter-in-law? What is the occasion?'

'You haven't been eating well, Mai. You look thin and pale.' Bhaunri kept her eyes fixed on the platter.

'I was never fat, daughter. And when have you seen me eating more or less?'

Bhaunri remained quiet for a moment. 'It is different these days. For you,' she said at last.

Mai looked at the young woman breaking pieces of roti carefully. 'It is different for you too, Bhaunri. Perhaps you would like to go to your parents' home? Girls return to their mairo in Saavan. It is the end of Bhadon now. What must your mother think...'

'Don't worry about me. I am happy with him.' She cast a sidelong glance at Mai and pitied her for not knowing the joy she herself was steeped in. A shiver ran through her at the memory of Bheema's warm body.

Mai reached out and caressed Bhaunri's head. 'They say that eyes that are too beautiful turn blind, and love that is too deep gets broken.'

'Not Bheema's and mine.' Bhaunri smiled, the corners of her lips curving deep into her cheeks.

Mai's eyes filled with tears, she continued to pat Bhaunri's head.

A MONTH HAD passed since the return of Bhaunri's father-in-law. Winter was approaching. At night, the shade of the mango tree felt like the cold water of a well.

'Why don't you two sleep indoors? It is so cold now,' Mai said one night.

Bhaunri was crushing turmeric and jaggery to mix with milk for the two men. 'Bheema says he sleeps outside until the water in the vats in our aangan freezes.'

'It may not have frozen over yet, but my hands turn numb when I draw water for the cows in the morning. He's a young man, he can sleep outside in all kinds of weather, but now he has to think of you.'

'I don't feel cold with Bheema there, Mai.' She stirred the sweet paste into the milk warming on the chulha.

'Take the camel-hair blankets from the storehouse then, the cotton sheet can't be sufficient. I will watch the milk,' Mai said after a pause.

Bhaunri nodded and stepped out of the kitchen. The storehouse was next to Mai's room. Blankets were stacked on a high shelf to protect them from rats. Bhaunri moved a trunk and stood on tiptoe to reach it.

'You want to break that beautiful surahi-like neck of yours by clambering on that rickety trunk, daughter-in-law?' She turned around. Her father-in-law was standing in the doorway. He entered the storehouse and lifted down the stack of blankets. 'Take the thick ones. Your young man can't keep you warm enough at night,' he mocked.

'Do you need blankets too, Sasura-ji? They won't warm your heart though.'

'Your words are like hot coals. They will keep me warm through the long winter night.'

Bhaunri picked two blankets and edged past him. He followed her out. 'I am not a thorn bush, daughter-in-law. Why do you shrink away? You think my touch is prickly?'

Bhaunri turned around and faced him squarely. 'Oh no, you are not the thorny one, father-in-law. It is I who am covered with thorns like a keekar tree. I am afraid I might tear you apart.'

He laughed loudly and looked over her shoulder at the pale face of his wife who had emerged from the kitchen carrying a tumbler of milk.

'What a tongue our daughter-in-law has! Her words are as sharp as her eyes. Why don't you learn from her, my wife?'

THAT NIGHT, RESTING against Bheema, running her fingers along the hard muscles of his arm, Bhaunri said, 'Is father-in-law going to stay long?'

'Why?' Bheema's muscles tensed under her fingers. 'What happened? He did something?'

'No ... But he talks nonsense sometimes. I told him if he doesn't stop, I will slit his throat one day.'

They lay in silence for some time. Bheema breathed heavily. 'I will crush him like a camel crushes an aak bush if he lays a finger on you,' he said through clenched teeth. 'I am not a milk-mouthed babe anymore. I will destroy him.' His voice rose. 'I will destroy him!'

Bhaunri was astonished. 'Don't worry, my dhani. It was nothing, just nonsense. He has a mouth that runs away from him.'

'It's not that, it is not just talk. He is a pret, that man, the unholiest of ghosts. He has come from a burning hell, and one of these days I will send him back there.'

'Don't speak like that, Bheema. He is your father.'

Bheema sat up. 'What do you know? You don't know anything. He is a pret. The only thing to do with him is to set him on fire so that everyone's freed of his evil presence. He has eaten through the family like a weevil hollows out grain. He drove Mangla to madness...' He ran out of breath. Bhaunri rubbed his back with the palm of her hand and handed him the pitcher of water. He took a gulp of cold water. 'Mai never speaks about it, but everyone knows what he did to her sister.' Bhaunri listened in silence. 'Her sister used to live with us. The house was so lively with her laughter and singing. She was a great help to Mai too. She looked after the cows, fed and played with Mangla and me. One day, when I was six or seven and Mangla a little older, she killed herself. Mangla found her hanging in the cowshed. She had used that pret's turban to hang herself. Mangla lost his wits that day. Now, whenever he manages to get out of his room, he runs to the corner of the shed where he had found her hanging and rages at her absence.'

'Why did she kill herself?'

'Why? Because he plagued her day and night, wouldn't leave her alone. He was always after her, following her, troubling her. We saw it all, Mangla and I.'

'Didn't Mai do anything?'

'What could she do? He is her husband. It would have been all right if it was any other woman – a man could have another woman, that is allowed. But this was her own sister. She put her odhani at his feet once, but he was like a camel in heat. No one, either in the family or the village, would help her or admonish him. Everyone was scared of him.' He drank some more water and wiped his mouth. 'I was a mere boy then. But it is different now. If he so much as raises his eyes to look at you, I will blind him. I will show him. I will show him!' His voice rose again, his body shook, the knuckles of his curled fists cracked.

Bhaunri took him in her arms. 'He can't do anything. We are joined at the heart, you and I, my dhani. Look here.' Her voice was like cool desert sand. 'I want to see your eyes. I was thinking of them when the sun struck the water in my pitcher this afternoon, and again when the moon rose. Look, how the mirrors on my kanchali sparkle. They remind me of your eyes too.'

Bheema's body slowly relaxed. He turned to her, into her, his rough caresses falling on her like the desert wind.

7

BHAUNRI ENTERED THE KITCHEN to find her mother-in-law wrapping rotis, onions and chillies in a piece of cloth.

'Your father-in-law is leaving,' she said, slipping a large pat of white butter between the rotis.

'Is he going away on his travels again?'

'Chhori, I don't ask questions. He tells me, "Pack some food, I am leaving," I pack the food and ask for God's blessings to keep him safe.'

Bhaunri picked up the milking pail and left the kitchen.

After the hustle of his departure was over, Bhaunri and her mother-in-law sat on the house-steps in the brief shade of the overhanging thatch and sewed in silence. Bhaunri was helping her mother-in-law stitch a new set of clothes. She herself still wore the clothes her own mother had made. The long blouses and skirts her mother-in-law had given her hampered her arms and tripped her when she walked.

'I heard Bheema shout last night. Was he angry at you?' Mai asked.

Bhaunri raised her sun-filled eyes. 'At me? No, he wasn't angry at me.' She smiled her secret smile. 'He's never angry at me.'

'Daughter-in-law, I am his mother. I carried him in my womb for nine months and tore my body to birth him and I am telling you, don't be so certain of him. He changes like the weather. Men do.'

'Perhaps.' Bhaunri caught the extra thread between her teeth and broke it off. 'My mother said to me that, before all else, hearts must meet. Unless hearts meet, everything else is a burden of sin and must be thrown off.'

Mai looked down at the piece of cloth she was embroidering and pierced it with the long needle she held. 'Mine had told me to tie an earthen pot to my neck and jump in the well if I ever so much as thought of complaining about my husband. I have always been afraid of wells.'

'But you are afraid of my father-in-law too. Are wells more fearsome than him? The desert is vast, it reaches the horizon. There is room for everyone here. Why would you live in fear?'

'There is more than one way for hearts to meet, Chhori. Sometimes they are twisted together, hurting each other but inseparable. You are a child. I pray your happiness thrives, but you must not let go of everything at once and become so immersed. I am afraid for you. You must keep safe.'

'Where is the question of safety between him and me, Mai? I must not think of safety. You know the story of the princess who followed the peacock? She had to follow him, whether he led her to the cloud palace or to a pit full of serpents.'

WITH THE FATHER-IN-LAW away, the household slid back into its old rhythms. Bheema stayed away some nights to look after the crops. On those nights, Bhaunri took the rough camel-hair blanket they slept under to Mai's room and wrapped herself in it.

'The old good-for-nothing didn't lift a straw, though he pretended he was looking after the crops. We will have the worst yield in the entire village this year,' Bheema grumbled when he returned in the morning, his eyes red, his face puffy with sleep. 'The cold bored holes into my bones last night, and that bitch of a wind kept blowing out the fire.'

Bhaunri gave him hot, milky tea to drink. She warmed some mustard oil, seasoning it with carom seeds, and rubbed the soles of his feet and his palms, his chest and back with it.

'My soul aches without you,' she said, looking up at him. 'Without your arms circling me, the night seems boundless. It is freezing. My heart trembles every moment. Take me with you.'

'You are mad. Where did you learn to talk such nonsense?' he said, smiling.

Bhaunri smiled too, though her heart felt full.

BHAUNRI SAT UNDER the mango tree embroidering Mai's new blouse. Mai herself was busy in the cowshed. Bhaunri held a circular bit of mirror down with her thumb and sewed around it. The mirror caught the sun and gleamed through the thread filigree. A bright reflection hovered over Bhaunri's bent head.

Mai came into the courtyard. Her odhani was awry and her hair was stuck to her forehead with sweat. 'Dhauli is having such a tough time calving ... The poor beast, she is trying so hard...'

Bhaunri looked up. The glowing reflection slid down her cheek and vanished. 'You want me to help, Mai? You look tired.'

'No, girl. She needs to do it herself, but I must be with her in the cowshed to help. You'll need to manage the evening chores by yourself.'

Bhaunri nodded. She folded the clothes, rose and fetched water and jaggery.

Mai took small bites of the sweet and sipped water. 'The poor creature is straining as hard as she can, while the ox is roaming the streets ... A woman's lot is always pain.'

Bhaunri smiled. 'Have you forgotten how restless she was before mating? Bheema had to get the bull for her urgently from the neighbouring village.'

'Yes. That's what I mean. Pain before and pain after, poor female.' She rose with a grimace and returned to the cowshed.

Bhaunri went indoors and began preparations for the evening meal. She filled a large aluminium pot with water and looked inside the bin containing the bones and scraps of meat for dog food.

'Mai, there's very little meat for his dogs,' Bhaunri called from the threshold of the shed. Mai was bent over the cow, massaging its bulging abdomen. 'Shall I get some from the Khateek's shop? I know where it is.'

The cow mooed in pain and Mai massaged harder. Bhaunri waited for a moment and then turned.

THE MEAT SHOP was at the other end of the village. It was actually a part of the butcher's home. In the front courtyard of the house, under a tin sheet resting on two wooden poles, was a rough wooden plank. On it stood a pair of scales and a slab of meat covered with a bit of stained cloth. From iron hooks fixed in the tin roof, hung carcasses of goats. There was no one in the shop. Bhaunri went up to the main house and called.

A young woman came to the house-door. She was short and plump, her pale complexion and small features were pretty but already dulled by the desert sun.

'What do you want?'

'I came to get some meat but there was no one in the shop.'

'My father is away. I'll give you the meat.' She accompanied Bhaunri to the shop. 'What do you need?' She picked up a long sharp knife and whetted it on a bit of stone.

'Just some meat and bones for the dogs.'

'I have not seen you before...'

'I am the daughter-in-law of the Lohars from the big house. I have not been in this village for a year yet.'

The woman looked up. She examined Bhaunri closely, curiously. 'You are Bheema's beendani?'

Something in her voice caused Bhaunri's back to stiffen. 'Yes. You know him? Perhaps you have seen him when he comes to buy meat here?'

The woman continued to stare at Bhaunri. 'I know him well,' she said slowly. 'He told me he brought you home a few months ago. He didn't want to bring you, but his mother nagged him day and night. He didn't want to have anything to do with you.'

'He said all that to you?' Bhaunri asked. 'Why to you? Who are you?'

The woman smiled a little. 'I am the Khateek's daughter. I have known Bheema for a long time.' She turned her eyes to the slab of meat, raised her knife and added, 'For a very long time. He comes here often.' She cut a thick slice and wrapped it in a bit of paper. 'Here.' She handed the parcel to Bhaunri. 'I will fetch the bones, they are in the backyard. I always keep them for his dogs.' She went into the house.

Bhaunri stood frozen for a moment and then, turning, she ran out, tears streaming down her cheeks. The village women saw her running through the streets, her head uncovered, the odhani slipping to her shoulders, muttering to herself. 'First, mad Mangla, and now this crazy bride,' they shook their heads. 'Poor Bheema's Mai, her fate is blighted.'

MAI MET HER in the courtyard. 'Dhauli came through at last. A she-calf too! But she suffered so much...' she began. Then she saw the tear-marks on Bhaunri's cheeks. 'What happened? Where had you gone?'

The parcel of meat slipped from Bhaunri's hands. She repeated the words she had been saying to herself, 'How is it possible? How? No, it is not possible.'

Mai took her arm and led her indoors. She made her drink some water and wiped her cheeks. 'Daughter-in-law, bear up. Whatever it is, bear up. It is the way of the world. You have to suffer like all of us.'

'Mai, our hearts are one, I know that. He knows it too. Then why? Why does he have to go to that woman?'

'Who knows why? Why does the sandstorm blow or scorpions sting? It is in their nature, that's all. What can you do? You are a woman. We are no different from Dhauli, our share is suffering and pain.'

'No, my share is the same as his. He and I are two parts joined together. How could his share be different from mine? I shall not suffer, Mai. If I do, so shall he.' Bhaunri's throat filled with sobs.

Mai rose wearily and lit the fire. 'Fetch the meat. He will be here soon. The dog food should be ready before that.'

Before Bhaunri could move, the street-door opened. 'Woman, I am home. Bring me water.'

Mai jerked her head up. 'Your father-in-law is back...'

Bhaunri sat up straight and wiped her face with the end of her odhani. Moving closer to the chulha, she pulled the platter of flour close and began kneading.

AT NIGHT, BHAUNRI cleaned the kitchen slowly. Her body felt weighed down, each action needed effort. Every few moments, she forgot what she was doing. She felt shut in an airless space, her breath coagulated inside her. The woman appeared before her. Her eyes pierced Bhaunri, her voice sounded in her ears. Sitting back on her haunches, she smote her forehead hard with her bunched fist again and again. Her tears fell into the ashes she was scrubbing the utensils with.

Gritting her teeth, she rose at last and, leaving the ash-smeared utensils unwashed, stepped out into the courtyard. Bheema was lying on his back, gazing up into the leaf-filled darkness.

Without turning his head, he said, 'What took you so long? You think I have nothing to do and you are the chief queen of Mewar that I have to stay up half the night waiting for you?' Then he turned, making room for Bhaunri on the cot. 'I had to go to the fields tonight but couldn't leave.' He lowered his voice. 'You must have bewitched me, you dakan. Come here. Why are you standing so far? Come, my beauty, it can't be the monthly problem yet.'

He reached out a hand towards her. She struck it away with the edge of her palm. Bheema looked at her, astounded.

'It is not the monthly problem. It is a different problem, of a far longer duration,' she said through clenched teeth. 'I met her. The Khateek's daughter.'

'So?'

'So? She is old and shapeless and pale like a sand dune, and she boasted to me that she knows you, that you visit her often.'

Bheema shook with laughter. 'Arre bawal, how does it matter? The Khateek's daughter is the Khateek's daughter. You are my wife. Your place is separate.'

Bhaunri groaned. His admission felt like the red hot brand with which her father used to brand cattle. 'I will not bear it, Bheema. I am not Mai. My mother...'

Bheema rose swiftly and was upon her before she could complete her sentence. 'Your mother was given far too much rope by your father. You take me for an impotent or a fool? You think you can make me dance if you raise your little finger? You dare compare yourself to my mother?'

Bhaunri pushed him with all her strength. 'No, I don't. I am not her. I am my mother's daughter. I won't bear this.'

She could hear Bheema grind his teeth. He pushed her to the ground. Bhaunri fought back, twisting her neck, jabbing at the insides of his arms with her elbows, kicking him with her silver-laden feet. He pressed with his full weight on her and pinned both her arms above her head.

'I did not want to bring you home because that pret had made our match. But Mai wouldn't let me live in peace, so I came to your village to fetch you. But then I saw you standing in your father's courtyard...' Bheema's rough voice grew low, his mouth was close to Bhaunri's ear. 'You were tall and shadowy like this mango tree, and you entered my heart against my will. But I am your man. You can't tie me to your skirt-strings. You are a woman, never forget that!'

His weight was on her stomach, on her chest. It caused Bhaunri's breath to come in shallow gasps. She could not speak, could not move, as Bheema entered her with force.

She lay awake after Bheema fell asleep. Her limbs ached, her body was sore. Hot tears seared her skin. When dawn reddened the sky, she rose. Her eyes burnt, her head felt hot. Filling a tumbler with cold water from the vat, she splashed it on her eyes and forehead.

'You need cold water on this freezing morning, daughter-in-law? Did Bheema fall asleep last night?'

She turned. It was her father-in-law. She averted her eyes and crossed the courtyard towards the house. She tried to hold herself straight, but her legs trembled and she stumbled on the house-steps. Her father-in-law was by her side in a flash. He helped her up.

'Clearly, I was wrong about Bheema.' He looked closely at her swollen eyes and drooping body. 'And perhaps about you too.'

Bhaunri's bosom heaved. She shook his hand off.

8

Bhaunri and Mai were preparing dinner for the household when they heard raised voices.

Mai listened for a moment, her elbow resting on an upraised knee, hand cupped around her ear. 'That's your father-in-law and Bheema. Hai Baba.' She joined her palms in supplication and bowed towards the niche in the wall where images of the patron deity of their village, Ramsha Pir, were displayed. 'I will light five diyas every Wednesday at your shrine. Don't let them fight, Baba.' Turning to Bhaunri, she said, 'Go, see what's the matter. I pray they don't come to blows...'

Bhaunri stepped out to the courtyard. Her father-in-law was squatting on the threshold, smoking his long hookah, and Bheema was standing in front of him. He was rolling his shoulders and flexing his arms.

'You lowlife, you sold all the goods you had brought from the town? You said you would let me have some for the shop. I could have got a good price for them, people from ten villages come to the shop now, but you sold everything to other shopkeepers.' The veins in his neck stood out. 'God's curse on you, you son of a widow.'

The older man continued puffing at his pipe vigorously. Bhaunri could hear the sound of bubbles whirling and popping in the bowl of the hookah from where she stood.

'You can't keep your word. It is not in you to keep your word,' Bheema added.

Bhaunri's father-in-law put his hookah aside and rose. He was a full head taller than his son, and his shoulders were as broad as a plough. 'Chhorey,' he said, his large eyes resting lightly on his son. 'Chhorey, do not speak to me in this way. Your new bride stands there listening. If I reply, it won't do your meagre manhood any favours.' He raised his turbaned head. 'And don't talk to me of keeping my word. I am a Gadoliya Lohar. I am the only one in this effeminate clan who has kept his nomadic vow. I never rest fully on the earth, I don't sleep on a cot, nor eat from a metal platter, I don't remain in one place, I go from town to village. Despite what the folk around here say, I can still work my forge if someone needs an iron implement. I sold my goods because I got a good price for them and respect for myself. If you want stock for your shop, stop wasting your time with worthless women from all over the village and go to the town to buy them yourself. The city is not far and travel is what nomads do, not fuck every prostitute in the village in broad daylight.'

'You are teaching me? You are telling me to stay away from women, you who fuck anything with a woman's parts? You accursed animal, you who didn't even spare your own sister-in-law?'

'You have grown muscular like a bull and have its brains too. In our clan, we marry a sister-in-law. Now get out of my way. Your bitter shadow has ruined my tobacco.' He picked up his hookah and brushed his son aside. At the street-door, he paused and looked at his son. 'I did not have a woman like your wife at home. If I had, I wouldn't have looked at another woman ever, even if a beauty from Inder's court stood before me,' he said and stepped out.

'You old good-for-nothing!' Bheema shouted after him. 'You will get it from me one of these days. One day I will kill you!' His restless glance fell on Bhaunri who stood stock still on the house-steps. He looked away. 'Old, conscienceless liar,' he muttered.

Bhaunri drew in a long breath. The strings of her kanchali dug into her back, her ivory bangles caught at her elbows, her ankle bracelets felt like bands of lead around her feet. With a heavy step, she crossed the courtyard and went up to her husband.

Bheema had picked up a pair of heavy wooden clubs and was twirling them, still muttering to himself, working off his fury.

'Why did he say that, Bheema?'

'Woman, go inside. I am mad with anger right now. There's murder on my mind. Get away from me.'

'On mine too. I feel I can rip my heart out of my breast and crush it with my two hands. You still go to all sorts of women? You said our hearts are melded as one, yours and mine...'

'What has gotten into your head? How dare you ask me questions? You are my wife. Haven't I told you not to forget your place?'

'But where is that place? Among the prostitutes you sleep with?'

Bheema roared like a bull. His wooden club hit Bhaunri's left shoulder with a thump. Burning pain shot through her shoulder, her arm. She swayed, her knees caved in like they were made of soft cotton, she couldn't feel her back. She stood, wavering like a shadow.

'I told you to hold your tongue. You have no control. Women are the root of all ills.' Bheema threw the clubs down and headed towards the door.

With her uninjured arm, Bhaunri reached over and picked up one of the clubs. Breathing shallowly, she hurled it with all her might towards Bheema. It struck the doorpost with a loud report like that of a rifle-shot. The flying wooden splinters struck Bheema.

Mai came running out. 'What happened? What was that sound? Hai Baba, daughter-in-law, daughter-in-law...' She bent over Bhaunri whose legs had finally given way. 'Hai Ram! Her shoulder is dislocated. Run, Bheema, call your father. It needs to be set immediately.'

Bheema moved towards the door, his eyes fixed on Bhaunri's motionless form. 'Is she ... is she breathing?'

'Lada, go. Get your father. She will be all right.'

But there was no need to go fetch him. Bhaunri's father-in-law had reached only as far as the street corner. On hearing the loud sound coming from his house, he had turned back. Now he entered the courtyard.

'What happened here? What's wrong with the girl?'

'Her shoulder ... Please see.'

Bhaunri's father-in-law turned her over and supported her into a sitting position. Bhaunri's head drooped, her body sagged.

'She is unconscious. That's good. This will hurt.'

The old Lohar placed his hand, as big as a platter, between her shoulder-blades, and with the other hand he wrenched the injured shoulder back into its socket. Bhaunri trembled and screamed.

'There, it is done. It is back in the right place. But it is going to hurt like an armful of cactus thorns. Daughter-in-law, can you bear it, or shall I get you some opium?'

Bhaunri sank her teeth into her lip and shook her head. A wave of nausea hit her as she tried to get up. She gagged and retched. Mai held her gently. With a tremendous effort of will, she rose, first to her knees and then to her feet. Her father-in-law looked on admiringly.

'She is some woman. Bheema, you fool, why did you hit her?'

'She wouldn't hold her tongue...'

'So you hit her with the mugdar and broke the chaukhat too?'

'She threw the mugdar at the chaukhat...'

'Next time I will aim for his head,' Bhaunri said between gasps.

'By God, I believe her too. Be careful, son, do not provoke her. She is some woman,' her father-in-law repeated. 'Take her inside now and give her some hot milk. Her shoulder should be kept warm. This will take weeks to heal. You sure you don't want the opium, daughter-in-law? The pain will increase as the injury cools.'

Bhaunri turned and, with Mai's help, walked towards the house. Bheema saw drops of blood fall from her lip where she had bitten it hard. He bent down and picked up the club and snapped it in two on his thigh.

FOR A WEEK, Bhaunri barely left the small room on the other side of Mai's kothari. She lay on a mattress, and for the first few days, no matter how many blankets Mai covered her with, trembled with cold. Mai looked after her, staying by her side night and day, heating bundles of cloth filled with grain to foment the injured arm, giving her hot milk and turmeric to drink. She called the ojha to chant his magic formulae and run his bundle of soft twigs over Bhaunri's shoulder to propitiate the spirits of pain.

Bhaunri's father-in-law came once a day to check on her. He loosened the bandage swaddling her shoulder and moved her arm up and down and sideways. Bhaunri set her teeth and bore the pain, moaning only occasionally.

Bheema, too, came to her sick-room, bringing tonics and strengthening potions. He placed them by her side. 'Take these, I got them from the doctor in the town,' he said in a low voice. She did not answer.

Mai's heart ached at the sight of her son's troubled eyes as he stepped out of the kothari. 'Your wife is getting better, Lada,' she assured him. 'She'll be out and about soon.' Bheema went away wordlessly. To Bhaunri, she said, 'He is not eating or sleeping properly. He is repenting, his heart is changing.' Bhaunri looked at her with fevered eyes and remained silent.

WHEN HER FEVER subsided, Mai allowed Bhaunri to come to the kitchen and sit by the chulha in the evening, but would not permit her to do any housework.

'No, no. You are not to touch the rolling pin or the water pot, daughter-in-law,' she said, gently pushing her away.

'What would your mother say if she heard I made her daughter work while ill and in pain?'

'Mai, my own mother would not have coddled me like this. You are treating me like I am a tender betel leaf.'

'There will be a time when you'll need to look after me, daughter-in-law. May that time be far away and may I not be a burden to you...'

Bhaunri's father-in-law saw her when he returned home. 'You are lucky that I was at hand to fix your shoulder. It would have taken some time for the pehelvan in the neighbouring village to come, and the shoulder would have frozen by then. Setting a cold injury is difficult.' He prodded the now-unbound shoulder with his finger. Bhaunri grit her teeth but did not wince. 'You've healed well, daughter-in-law. Now go and rest.' To his wife he said, 'I will get some herbs. Give it to her every day with milk.'

'Your father-in-law is famous for setting broken bones. His name is respected in ten villages,' Mai told her later.

'And for breaking bones too?'

Mai smiled a half smile. 'You are better now. That long tongue of yours is wagging again. Yes, he was famous for breaking bones too. He used to win every wrestling competition. People flocked from all over the tehsil to see him. He fought two, sometimes three opponents at the same time. He had this trick of pressing a nerve and immobilizing his opponent within moments...' She sighed as she rose. 'But all the skill will be lost with him. He hasn't taught anyone ... Perhaps it is better that way...'

As Bhaunri's shoulder healed, she moved around the house and did some light housework. Bheema saw little of her. She retreated to her room before he returned in the evening, and slept indoors.

EARLY ONE MORNING, a few weeks after her injury, Bhaunri came out to the house-steps. Bheema had just woken up and was sitting on his string cot, chewing a neem twig. He watched her as she stretched, the curved lines of her body were like the markings of wind on sand dunes. She drew out an acacia twig from the fold of her ghaghra and chewed on it as she walked across the courtyard towards him.

It was the month of Kartik, of dry-edged cold winds and the onset of night-frost. A thin film of ice had formed on the water in the vat. Bhaunri filled a brass tumbler and took an icy mouthful. Rinsing her mouth, she spat the water and refilled the heavy tumbler.

'Here, take.' She held it out to Bheema.

Bheema took it. He also gargled and spat. The early morning light fell on Bhaunri, burnishing her skin. 'Your arms gleam like a snake and they strike like a snake too,' he said. 'You could have split my head with that mugdar.'

'Are you complaining that I didn't? Give me another occasion, Baalam, and I will.' She extended her arm. 'Look, my arm's fine now, as strong as ever.'

Bheema touched her arm. The cloth of her kanchali rustled under his palm. He bent and rubbed his wet mouth on her shoulder. Bhaunri smiled, her eyelids drooped, and she swallowed the lump in her throat.

The sun had come up behind the mango tree. Bhaunri turned back towards the house. At the house-steps stood her father-in-law, his turbanless head touching the thatch. Bhaunri looked at him unflinchingly as she passed into the house.

9

While Bhaunri recovered, besides caring for her, Mai had to shoulder the burden of running the entire household. She looked tired all the time and, though she never complained, her sighs when she bent or straightened were deep. When her shoulder healed completely, Bhaunri relieved Mai of as many household tasks as she could. She prepared the morning meal for Bheema and her father-in-law, milked the cows, churned curd and swept the house and courtyard. She warmed oil for her father-in-law and kept his bathwater ready. Still, Mai had her hands full.

Looking after Mangla had suddenly become difficult. Usually silent and manageable, he banged on the door of his room in the middle of night, screamed incoherent abuses from the narrow window, and threw his food. In the mornings, Mai could no longer take him out to the open patch behind the house to relieve himself. He would run away from her or fling excrement around. Bheema had to accompany him and threaten him with a heavy stick.

Once, he escaped from the house and ran through the village, shrieking at the top of his voice. It caused such a commotion that the Sarpanch suggested it was perhaps time to send Mangla to the asylum in Jaipur. Mai spoke up for the first time in a gathering of the community elders then. 'I will hang myself and him in the cowshed rather than send him to the asylum to be beaten senseless by the santaris and given electric shocks until he loses all traces of humanity,' she said.

BHAUNRI WAS MILKING the cows when she heard a loud sound. Mangla had managed to break the latch of his room's door. He came up to where she was crouched beside a cow. She stiffened and braced herself but did not stop milking. Her fingers continued to press the teats and send jets of milk into the bucket clamped between her knees. Mangla stood regarding Bhaunri for a few moments and then ran towards the courtyard letting out whoops.

Bhaunri followed him, unsure whether Bheema or her father-in-law were around to guide him back. Mangla ran about shouting. He scattered the red chillies set out for drying and knocked the utensils over. Then he caught sight of the three-coloured turban hanging on the clothesline. With a piercing scream, he snatched it and, throwing it on the ground, trampled it under his feet, rubbing it into the dust.

Mai came hurrying out from the house. 'Mangla, tabur,' she called out. 'My son, don't.' She took him by the arm and, speaking softly, led him back towards the cowshed.

'Wife, I need my safa.' Bhaunri's father-in-law entered the house.

Mangla stopped at the sound of his voice and, shaking off Mai's restraining hand, ran screaming towards him, his fists clenched, his mouth foaming. The older man was taken by surprise but managed to subdue him, grabbing Mangla in a fierce embrace as he forced him back towards the shed. Bhaunri stood watching as Mangla struggled with mad strength. The two moved in a reluctant synchrony, like an ungainly four-legged creature, towards the little room. Mangla turned his head towards his mother and screamed, his eyes wild with fear.

Bhaunri was moved to tears. 'Don't worry, Jeth-ji, don't worry.' She reached out and caressed his rough head. 'Everything's all right. I will be milking the cows right here. You go in and rest.'

Mangla's screams subsided into whimpers. Mai followed father and son into the little room.

'Mangla is always difficult when that pret is around,' Bheema said when Bhaunri told him about the morning's episode. 'Even if he doesn't see my father, he somehow knows he is present. And when he sees him, he goes completely out of control. I wish the old sinner would leave us in peace and never return.'

'Don't worry. Mangla was like a baby afterwards. I gave him milk and roti with sugar this evening. He ate so quietly. He likes to see me in the cowshed too. He is always at the window when I am milking.'

'You are a dakan.' Bheema pulled her into his arms. 'You have bewitched us all.'

Bhaunri's teeth flashed in the dark.

WINTERS WERE PROGRESSING steadily though somewhat slowly, when Bhaunri decided to prepare a special winter lunch for Bheema one afternoon. She made rotis of gram flour and millet mixed with jaggery, and cooked bitter methi leaves to balance the sweetness. Wrapping the hot rotis in a piece of cloth to keep them warm, she packed everything in a small straw basket along with an onion and some fresh green chillies, and tied the basket carefully in a piece of cloth, ready for the boy from the shop to carry it to Bheema.

At the sound of the street-door, she came out, but instead of the boy, the old bhishti stood in the courtyard, panting.

'I have run all the way from the fields, Beendani,' he gasped. 'Give me some flour, jaggery and ghee. Also some old sacks. And be quick! A big faka has arrived.'

'A swarm of locusts?' Mai joined Bhaunri in the courtyard. 'Has it landed?'

The bhishti nodded. 'Yes, in some fields. Yours are safe. The Nath Jogi arrived and chanted his prayers, and stopped the locusts from landing in your fields. Bheema has asked me to bring seedha for the Jogi's fee. Hurry please. Bheema will be angry if I don't get back quickly.'

The bhishti squatted by the threshold as Mai hurried to gather dry staples for the holy man who had stopped the locusts from destroying their field.

'So many are still circling that the sky is dark with them,' the bhishti said, gulping the water Bhaunri gave him. 'You can't hear a man calling because of their murmuring. This is the biggest faka I have ever seen. Kalbelias are catching them, but they don't have enough sacks to put them in.'

Mai brought flour, jaggery, ghee and sacks from the storeroom.

'Mai, I'll take them.' Bhaunri rose. 'I have never seen a swarm of locusts. And look how tired he is. He won't be able to reach the fields quickly.'

The bhishti settled down comfortably, leaning against the door, and began rubbing chewing tobacco on his palm. 'Yes, yes, go. The faka is a sight to see. May God grant that we don't see it too often.'

'But it is far, daughter-in-law. Besides, Bheema might not like you going there...'

'No, no, let her go, let her go. Other women from the village will be there too, to sing the song of the locusts,' the bhishti said, coating his gums with tobacco and easing his goatskin water-carrier to the floor.

BHAUNRI TOOK THE sacks from Mai's hands and ran out of the house. Even before she reached the fields, she could see the dark, cloud-like swarm of locusts hovering low over the fields. The air was filled with a strange rustling, and the sharp green smell of crushed insects was everywhere. There were people in the fields, moving between rows of growing crops. She recognized the Kalbelia women and men by their dark clothes. Village folk were beating brass platters to scare away the locusts which had not yet landed, and were lending a hand to the Kalbelias in collecting the insects which had already settled on the plants. A Nath Jogi, with heavy stone earrings pulling his earlobes down to his shoulders, was seated cross-legged on the mud wall of a field and was chanting loudly, holding his curled fist skyward.

Bhaunri walked with a quick step towards her husband's fields. She looked for Bheema amongst the Kalbelias and Nats as she distributed the sacks to them. At last she spotted him in a neighbouring field, bent over a row of plants. 'Bheema,' she called. Bheema turned, and she sprang across irrigation ditches and skirted rows of wheat plants as high as her waist to reach him.

As she approached, a woman rose beside Bheema. She was holding a cloth sack. She took hold of Bheema's hand and shook the locusts he held in his palms into her sack. Then she turned her pale face towards Bhaunri and smiled.

Bhaunri stopped, her feet stuck to the ground, her leather mojaris felt like traps. Bheema shook off the Khateek's daughter's hand and came towards her.

'What are you doing running about in the fields? Who told you to come?'

'I brought seedha for the Jogi, and sacks. And I wanted to see the swarm.' Bhaunri spoke with effort, her throat was dry.

'There is nothing to see, this is not a fair. Locusts are just pests.' He looked back at the Khateek's daughter. 'What are you grinning like a fool about, woman? Go on, collect the locusts before they eat the ears of wheat.' Turning back towards Bhaunri, he took the sackful of staples from her and said, 'Go back home. You have seen enough now, haven't you?'

'Let me stay and collect them with you.' Bhaunri's eyes seemed darker under the midday sun.

'O fortunate one, you don't need to get your hands dirty touching these creatures. They smell, and it is backbreaking work collecting them, not a game.' He looked away from her and across the rows of crop. 'Go home. I'll be back once the fields are cleared and the swarm is chased away.' He turned and walked back towards the Khateek's daughter.

Bhaunri turned too. She walked blindly, stubbing her feet against stones, stumbling as she crossed the low mud-boundary of the field. She looked back and saw her husband speaking to the woman beside him. The woman covered her mouth with the end of her yellow headscarf and laughed.

MAI WAS IN the kitchen when Bhaunri returned. 'You are such a careless girl, you just rushed off. I called after you to take his meal too.'

'He won't need this food, he has food there.'

'Where? At the field?'

'Yes, the Khateek woman is there. She will feed him.' Bhaunri's eyes were dry and fiery like the month of Jeth. 'He eats there from time to time, doesn't he, Mai? That's why he doesn't come home to eat some days?'

Mai adjusted the wood in the chulha and rose to get the dry-leaf platters from the niche in the wall. 'Let's make rotis for your father-in-law. He will be home soon. He won't go to the fields to help drive the locusts away. Locusts are nomads like us he says, and he won't harm his brethren.'

Bhaunri went closer to her. 'You knew about this woman, Mai, didn't you? You've known about her all along. Has he been going to her for long? Is it only her he goes to when he disappears at night, or are there others too? Was my father-in-law telling the truth when he said he goes to prostitutes?' Mai sprinkled water on the platters and wiped them with the end of her odhani. 'You've known everything but you did not tell me, Mai.'

Mai raised her head. 'What good would have come from telling you, daughter-in-law? What can you do? You must learn not to take this so badly. He is a man after all, he'll do as he wishes. Before he brought you home, he had said to me that he would have nothing to do with you. "You are forcing me to bring her home, so you must look out for her," he told me. But now, see how he has taken you to heart? You are his wife, add to the family. Once children come, he will stop all this.'

'Did my father-in-law stop after you had children?'

Blood rose in Mai's pale face. 'Whatever your father-in-law did, I never complained. I accepted my fate. That is the only way.'

The street-door opened. 'There is excitement in the village today,' Bhaunri's father-in-law said as he entered the kitchen. 'Everyone is after the locusts. The Kalbelias and Nats have collected enough to last them as snacks for months now. And hardly any damage to the crops. Poor locusts.' He burst into song, 'O locust of slender feet and radiant colour, fly away for the men are after you. They will devour you, o locust of the lovely cheeks.'

Bhaunri turned away towards the chulha and Mai began serving him food.

'Why is it so quiet here? Two women and not a sound? Do neither of you know the song of the locusts? Even a funeral is more cheerful than this household.'

'Please eat your food, it is getting cold,' Mai said quietly.

'You, my daughter-in-law? Have you lost your tongue too? Your mother only taught you to slit throats, not to sing?'

Bhaunri flung her head up and turned. Her eyes fell on her father-in-law with an intensity that startled him. 'Whatever my mother taught me has been plain to everyone from the beginning, my sasura. But what did you teach your son? He keeps another woman under your nose. He shamelessly parades her before the whole village. He does not value his good name or keep my honour.'

Mai froze. For a moment, there was no sound in the kitchen except for Bhaunri's quick breath, like an echo of her words.

Finally, Bhaunri's father-in-law spoke. 'Daughter-in-law, you have no cause for complaint. As long as he keeps you in his home, he is doing his duty as a husband. If you want more, if you are burning because he has another, make it your business to let him know. It is not for me to interfere with a grown son, though he be ever so stupid. What's between a man and his wife must remain so. Now take that roti out of the chulha before it turns into coal.' He began eating his food.

10

Bheema didn't come home that night, or the next. The boy from his shop did come with a message, though. 'He will sleep in the fields. Other swarms have been sighted in neighbouring villages.' Mai gave the boy food and blankets, a set of clothes and Bheema's chillum. 'Come back if he needs anything else,' she told him.

Bhaunri went about her chores at home in silence, her body tense, her gaze abstracted. Bheema's absence was like an open wound. Every moment she felt that the pain would spill out of her like blood, flooding the house, engulfing the village, drowning the world.

The second evening of Bheema's absence, Bhaunri's father-in-law returned before sundown. He sat on the house-steps, smoking his hookah and watched her going to and fro in the house.

'Daughter-in-law,' he called as she fetched water for preparing the evening meal. 'Come here, listen to an old sinner's advice. Don't look like this, like a rain-filled cloud. Anger can be beautiful in love, but not this heavy, wordless sullenness.' He looked at her with his bloodshot eyes. 'You are a matchless woman, your eyes are like stars and your mouth like a ripe mulberry fruit. You glow and ripple like the fire in the sea. Use this anger to fuel love. There's nothing like love to keep a man, and nothing like love to drive him away too. You need to know which kind keeps him and which drives him away. And no tears. What good are tears? They make eyes which should droop with love puffy. Who can enjoy a weeping woman?'

Bhaunri's heart swelled in her chest. 'You advise me, father-in-law, but what about him? Is a man taught about the kind of love that keeps a woman, that makes her eyes droop, not because she wishes to please him, but because she is pleased in her heart? Do men only know the khota kind of love, spurious like a gilt ornament, which only pleases the eye for a few days? Not the real kundan which shines brighter as time passes? Don't teach me about love, father-in-law. What do you know about it? Your wife trembles at your footstep. That is not love. Love doesn't fear anything, it doesn't even fear losing love itself.'

Her father-in-law looked away from her with difficulty. He drew a long breath. 'You catch fire like dry straw, daughter-in-law. Take care, one of these days you will burn everything down.'

BHEEMA RETURNED LATE on the third evening. He looked tired, his eyes swollen from interrupted sleep. He washed and came into the kitchen to eat. Mai set out his platter and poured melted ghee on his roti.

'You worked too hard, my son. Your face is tanned and your cheekbones jut out. Who knows what you ate...'

'Don't worry, I didn't starve. I had plenty to eat,' Bheema answered.

Bhaunri's eyes flared but she kept her lips pursed and crisped a roti for him.

'She has learnt to make roti like you, Mai. Look how crusty this one is.'

'Indeed. She learns everything quickly. You are fortunate, my son.'

Bheema turned his eyes towards Bhaunri and smiled a smile that pierced her.

After the evening's work was over and the kitchen tidied, Bhaunri came out into the courtyard. Bheema was sitting on the string cot.

'It is getting colder. Soon we'll need to sleep inside the house,' he said and pulled her by the arm on to the cot. They lay pressed against each other.

'It is colder here than in my father's village,' Bhaunri said.

'But surely you like it better here. In your father's village you only had quilts and the coal brazier, here you have me to keep you warm.' Bheema caressed her. 'What's your father's village compared to my arms?'

'My village has such sights to see. There are date palms and cheetal deer and peacocks aplenty, and desert partridge that feed in the thickets.'

Bheema held her tighter. 'There might have been black fawn and peacocks in that little forest near your village, but why make up stories? There is no such bird as a desert partridge. Partridges do not live in the desert.'

'They do too. I have laid traps for them along with my brothers.'

'If you did, the only thing caught in those traps must have been your lies! I know better than you. I have travelled as far as Jodhpur, and have spent months with the Raj Nats who go from village to village. I know all about the desert.'

'I don't tell lies. In my village, desert partridges are as common as Khateek girls are in yours.'

Bheema stiffened. The pressure of his arms on Bhaunri's body changed. 'You dare to speak like this? To mock me? Didn't you learn your lesson last time?'

'And didn't you learn yours?' Bhaunri hissed. 'To go brazenly to that woman, spend the past two nights with her, and then come to me as if nothing happened?'

Bheema shook with anger. He tightened his arms until pain shot through Bhaunri's left shoulder. She suppressed a cry and said, 'If you think you can scare me, Dhola, you mistake me for someone else.' She struggled against his restraining arms, sinking her teeth into his shoulder. Bheema yelped in pain and slapped her hard, breaking the skin on her face. Bhaunri's mouth filled with the metallic taste of blood. Raging, he grabbed her by the shoulders and threw her across the cot, rolling on top of her. The wooden frame of the cot pressed painfully into her back, her thighs.

'I only broke your shoulder last time. I will maim you if you don't watch what you say, don't think that I won't. You are just a woman, there are many like you. I will bring another and keep her right here in this house. What will you do then?'

'I will poison her, I will lie with any man that would have me, I will drag your shame into the village streets for all to see,' Bhaunri gasped.

Bheema pummelled her with his fists, raining blows on her shoulders and head until she lost consciousness. When she came to, she was lying flat on the cot. The blanket covered her body, every inch of which throbbed with pain.

'Here, drink some water.' Bheema held a heavy tumbler to her mouth. Bhaunri's lip was cut, she winced but took a few gulps. 'You awaken the demon in me with your thorny tongue. One day, I will really do something to you.'

He lay next to her and was soon fast asleep. The half moon shed its light on his sleeping form. His head turned sideways, his close-cropped hair like a shadow, his hands curled into fists and his face relaxed, he slept soundly.

Bhaunri tried to straighten her bruised limbs and a moan escaped from her lips.

MAI WAS AGHAST to see Bhaunri the next morning. 'Hai Baba, hai Baba,' she cried.

She made her sit by the chulha. Twisting bits of cloth into a ball, she warmed it over the iron griddle. 'Here, hold it against your cheek and mouth.' She roasted millet flour to make hot poultice with turmeric and carom seeds for Bhaunri's bruised arm and shoulder. 'Turn around and let me put this on you,' she said, muttering prayers under her breath.

'Give her ghee and turmeric in hot milk to drink. There might be some internal injuries too,' Bhaunri's father-in-law said as he entered the kitchen. 'Is it the same shoulder which was dislocated?'

'Yes, but it is not like last time,' Bhaunri said. Her swollen mouth moved in an unfamiliar way, and the words came out jumbled.

'Let me see it.' Bhaunri kept her eyes lowered as her father-in-law bent over and examined her shoulder and back. 'It is not broken. The bone sits nicely in the socket, but it is badly bruised. Give her the herbs I brought last time,' he said to his wife. Turning to Bhaunri he added, 'You are a very troublesome girl, daughter-in-law, throwing wooden clubs and sharp words around carelessly. Sleep indoors for a few days. These injuries are going to hurt like hot coals in this cold weather.'

Bhaunri looked up. Tears pooled in the corners of her eyes. Pain moved in a wave across her face. Leaning against the wall, she exhaled slowly. Her father-in-law stood watching her in silence for a moment.

'Look after her. Keep her warm,' he said at last, and walked away.

FOR THREE DAYS Bhaunri lay inside the house. Her body healed with the herbs and medicines her father-in-law brought every day. Her mother-in-law applied poultice and ghee on her injuries. Bheema didn't come near her at all. She didn't know whether he came home or spent his nights elsewhere. On the fourth day, Bhaunri rose from the bed. Her body still ached, but she felt strong enough to go about the household chores.

She was in the courtyard collecting papads put out to dry, when Bheema returned home. At the sound of the street-door, she raised her head and threw a dart-like glance at him. Then, her hands full of the paper-thin lentil wafers, she turned and went into the house, her body taut like a string. Later that night, Bhaunri made Bheema's bed in the kothari she slept in.

'She is not going to give in,' her father-in-law said to his wife as he watched Bhaunri go to and fro, carrying a pitcher, blankets, a cotton durrie. 'She is like Jesal-de who fought the witch from Bengal for her husband. You've heard the story the Nayaks recite? She was cut in two parts and burnt, but she caused the cinders to smoulder until summer arrived and then set the whole forest on fire and burnt the witch's haveli.'

'But Jesal-de was so foolish,' his wife said in a low voice. 'In the story she also burnt the entire village and her own husband.'

'She was magnificent. She was determined to not be parted from her husband, and the only way they could be together was if he too turned into ashes like her. You won't understand the fire that consumes lovers, wife, it is not in your nature.'

His wife bent her head and continued pressing his legs. Tears dripped from her eyes on to her kurti.

BHAUNRI HAD CLEANED the kothari earlier in the day and applied fresh lime to the walls. She had hung her elaborately beaded cloth-ring, with ropes of coloured beads hanging from it, on a nail in the wall next to a small mirror and a picture of Hanuman, the god of wrestlers. She tucked lit incense sticks under the god's image and placed the pitcher full of water on a metal trunk painted green and decorated with pink lotuses. Bheema sniffed appreciatively as he entered.

'It is not like the open aangan and the mango tree, but this is not bad.' He put his arms around her. 'You look like the velvet night outside. How can you be so beautiful, Chhori, and have such a poisonous tongue? I want to suck all your poison out.' He fastened his mouth on hers.

Later, as they lay together, their limbs entangled, Bhaunri said, 'I miss the rustling of the leaves and the sky above. The roof is like a lid.'

'I can't break the roof, my Moomal,' Bheema laughed, 'but tomorrow I will hang mango leaves here for you.'

'Tomorrow I will bring your lunch out to the fields myself and feed you with my own hands.'

Bheema shifted. 'No, it is best you stay at home. It is never certain where I am, at the shop or the fields or the akhada. You will waste your time looking for me. And anyway, I have too much to do during the day.'

'What are your afternoons busy with, my husband?'

'It is none of your concern, my woman.'

Bhaunri turned towards him. 'Why not? Take care, even sandalwood catches fire if rubbed too long.'

'Who is afraid of fire, girl? Fire is home and hearth, food and warmth, and the last refuge too. You are of this desert, better get used to burning fires. But why speak of fire? Why fight? If you search in ten villages you won't find someone like me, and if I look through the whole desert there won't be another one like you.' Bheema slid his palm along the curved, firm lines of her body. 'By the spirits of my ancestors, there's no one like you.'

Bhaunri wrapped herself around him, each plane and contour of her body moulding itself around his. 'See how we fit together, Baalam, like the pieces of a puzzle. If there is no one like me, then why are there others?'

'Don't pester me, woman. Don't question me. It will only lead to trouble.'

'I am not afraid of trouble. Love is the twin of trouble. If my heart hadn't belonged to you, there would be no trouble. I would have simply left you.'

Bheema held her throat in his two hands. 'I will snap your neck like a lotus stem if you so much as think of leaving me. The more I indulge you, the more querulous you get.'

11

MAI DECIDED TO GET the quilts refilled. 'The cotton-wool has lost its softness. These quilts are as hard as wooden planks. We need to send for the dhunia.'

She showed Bhaunri how to undo the stitches so that it would be easy to pull out the cotton. When all the quilts were opened, the dhunia would flay the cotton with his wood-and-metal-wire equipment which twanged like a sarangi, until the cotton was soft and fluffy again. As they sat working in the courtyard, the street-door flew open and a small child rushed inside.

'Kaki-sa, Kaki-sa! Dadi-sa has gone into a trance. Mother has said she will begin answering questions soon,' he announced, then ran back out.

Mai's face brightened. 'That was Nathi's grandson. Her son Sundar died five years ago from a snakebite. One night he got drunk and urinated unknowingly beside Goga-ji's shrine. Of course Goga-ji was angry and, that same night, he was bitten by a snake. Everyone prayed to Goga-ji to spare his life but the god did not heed their prayers. The poison soon reached his heart and, as he lay dying, he asked us to promise not to worship at the shrine of such a vindictive god. He vowed that if the entire village obeyed, he would visit the village after his death and solve problems, answer questions.'

'But you prayed to the snake god when the scorpion stung the black cow.'

'Of course we pray to him. You can't stop praying to such a mighty god just because he is ruthless. The village elders consulted a wise Bhopa who said only that particular shrine was proscribed. So we abandoned it and another one was built for Goga-ji. You can see that that has satisfied Sundar – he possesses his mother once in a while and answers all kinds of questions. I want to ask when I will be blessed with a grandchild.' Mai smiled, the eagerness on her face shone bright. 'And also about Mangla ... But your father-in-law might come for lunch. He will be angry if no one's home. And there's the dhunia, he is very free with his words. I can't leave you alone to deal with him...'

'You go, Mai. I will take care of everything. We can get the cotton flayed another time.'

Mai looked at her. 'I don't like to leave you behind, Beendani...'

'Mai, I am not made of sugar and wheat flour that a crow will eat me.' Bhaunri smiled. 'Now go before Sundar dyor-sa leaves.'

Mai rose hurriedly. At the street-door, she turned and asked softly, 'You want me to ask about Bheema...?'

'Ask what about him?'

'About that woman...'

'No. I don't need to ask anything.'

AFTER SHE FINISHED with the quilts, Bhaunri heaped them in a corner. She didn't feel like leaving the bright courtyard and going into the house. The winter sunshine soothed her aching body. She fetched a comb and mirror and, sitting with her back to the sun, undid her braids. Her shoulder felt stiff and painful. With clumsy movements, she began combing her hair. She did not hear the street-door open and was startled by the broad shadow falling over her. She turned, shading her eyes with her hand. Her father-in-law stood behind her. Her hand dropped, a grimace parted her lips.

'I can understand you are not overjoyed to see me, daughter-in-law. But there is no reason to look pained.'

Bhaunri rose. 'You are mistaken. It is my shoulder. It hurts. The food is ready. I will serve it for you.'

'Still hurts? It had set beautifully. Did he hurt you again?'

Bhaunri met her father-in-law's eyes. 'And what if he did? This is not the first time a man has hurt a woman in this house.'

'Ah, such flower-like words! If you can still sting like a green chilli, it can't be very bad.' He kept his eyes fixed on her.

'Bad or good, what is it to you, father-in-law? What is between a man and his wife must remain between them.' But her voice cracked and tears fell from her eyes.

'Sit down there, daughter-in-law.' He pointed to the string cot. 'Tie up your hair. Let me see your shoulder.' Bhaunri raised her arms to gather her hair. A groan escaped her. 'Let it be, let it be, girl. I will comb your hair for you.'

'You, father-in-law?'

He bent and picked up the comb. 'Yes. Now sit. Where is your mother-in-law?'

'She has gone to pray to Sundar dyor-sa's ghost and ask questions.'

'Typical. Asking a dead man when she should be looking to the living one for answers. You didn't go?'

'I know the answers to my questions already.'

Her father-in-law clicked his tongue as he took bunches of her hair between his fingers and plaited them. 'And what if the answers you know are all wrong?' Bhaunri remained silent. His large fingers were surprisingly nimble. After plaiting her hair, he gathered the numerous braids and, twisting and rolling them into an elaborate bun, secured them with iron hairpins. His fingers rested on the nape of her neck for a moment.

Bhaunri turned her head and looked at him with sun-dazzled eyes. 'How good you are at this, father-in-law! You do it better than anyone I know! Where did you learn to do hair so well?' Her odhani slipped off her shoulder. The curves of her breasts, her smooth back and wave-like waist were bared.

The old Lohar looked, transfixed. Then he shook his head, moving back a step. 'Better not ask, daughter-in-law. What is between a man and his hair-dressing teacher must remain so. Go, get me my food.'

Bhaunri pulled her odhani in place and went into the house.

BHAUNRI'S FATHER-IN-LAW BEGAN coming home for lunch more often. Mai noticed that after lunch, instead of leaving for the chaupal or the fields, he lingered in the courtyard, smoking his hookah. Bhaunri found the sunless house cold. She preferred cleaning grain or churning curd in the courtyard too. From time to time, she freshened her father-in-law's hookah or served him snacks. If he was in a chatty mood, he told her stories from his travels while she worked.

'I have seen snakes as thick as that cattle-rope you are mending, daughter-in-law, and longer than the length of this cot,' he told her one day. 'One coiled itself around my bullock's leg. I had to wrap my arms just below its gaping maw and pull with all my strength to get it off.'

'And what did you do once you got it off?' Bhaunri asked, threading the long, thick needle.

'I flung it as far away as I could. I had to be very quick or the beast would have coiled around me and that would have been the end.'

Bhaunri caught her lower lip between her teeth as she pressed the long needle into the thick coil of rope she was mending. Her arm trembled.

'Daughter-in-law, is your shoulder still giving you trouble? Is there still some weakness?'

Bhaunri succeeded in passing the needle through the rope and continued to stitch carefully.

'I have soaked some herbs in oil.' He pulled out a small bottle from the pocket of his jhagga. 'Here, take this. Massage your shoulder with it.'

Bhaunri looked up. 'I can't reach where it hurts. It is the back of my shoulder. I can't raise my arm. It even hurts when I milk the cows.'

'Oh. The injury has taken root. This is not good. It will hurt more and more every year. Old injuries don't heal by themselves, they get worse with time.'

Bhaunri's gaze wavered. 'I will ask Mai to rub the oil.'

'Ask Mai? What good would Mai do? You need an expert for this. The injury needs to be put right, or you will suffer all your life. Come here, I will massage your shoulder.' Bhaunri stepped across to where he sat on Bheema's cot. 'Let me see your shoulder. Don't be shy. I had set it last time and I am a haad-vaid, I have seen more shoulders, knees and backs than I can count.'

Bhaunri reached back, undid the top string of her bodice and, holding it to her breast with one hand, slipped it off her injured shoulder.

'There is a large bruise here. There must have been much internal bleeding,' her father-in-law said as he poured some oil into his palm. He began kneading and manipulating her shoulder. Bhaunri held herself rigid against the pain. 'I know it hurts now, but you will feel relief by tonight. The blood needs to be drained and the muscles and tissues massaged deeply. See how the sinews are all knotted up here?' He rubbed her arm and shoulder and back, pressing the firm flesh with his palms and knuckles. 'You know, daughter-in-law, you are very beautiful. I have not seen anyone like you, and I have seen many. Why do you fight with him? Youth resides in the body only for a short while, so why not enjoy it while it lasts? Give up fighting with Bheema. What you want, you can never gain by stubbornly asking for it again and again, so just take what you have been given. Trust me, I know. I drove the one I loved to death because of my stubbornness.'

'How can I give up, father-in-law? To give up would be to part my heart from his, and that would kill me.'

'I thought so too, once. But when I lost her, I saw what a fool I was. It would have been far better to let her go to another than to lose her altogether.'

'I know about Mai's sister. Bheema told me she hanged herself because of you – because you wanted her and she didn't love you.'

'Bheema is a fool. We loved each other from the day your mother-in-law brought her to this house after her family was hounded out from their village.'

'Hounded out? Why?'

'Because their mother had cursed the whole village in a fit of anger. Her husband was gored to death by a bull owned by the Brahmins. She was so devoted to her husband, she decided to commit sati with him and, from her pyre, she cursed the village: Just as her helpless husband was crushed, so shall their crops be destroyed. Just as no one gave him even a drop of water to drink when he lay dying, so there shall be no water for them.'

'And did her curse come true?'

'I don't know whether it was the curse, but that year herds of nilgai entered their village just as the maize and barley were ripe for harvesting, and before anyone could do anything, they destroyed the crops. Not even grain to eat could be salvaged from the ruined fields. Then the deepest well in the village ran dry. The Brahmins decreed that it was the spirit of the sati causing this trouble, and so the villagers boycotted their family. The men of the family, your mother-in-law's brothers, went to the city and became rickshaw-pullers. And Phoolan came to us ... She was truly a desert-flower. I wanted to marry her, but she said she won't be her sister's co-wife. "What will everyone say?" she asked every time we were together. "They'll say I am my own sister's saut, that I took away your love from her." And your mother-in-law made it worse. Crying night and day, begging her, praying, chanting, fasting. The entire village supported her and boycotted Phoolan. She begged me, "Let me go away from here, let me marry another," but I didn't listen. "Kill me before you take another man," I told her. She killed herself instead. If only I had not insisted, she would still be alive, even if in another house, as another man's wife...'

'That would never have done, father-in-law. There is no pain like the pain of separation when your heart is joined to another's. It is worse than all the hells the priest at the shrine speaks of.'

'You are a headstrong girl, Bhaunri. Go, your shoulder is done for today.'

Bhaunri rose and, reaching back stiffly with both hands, tried to tie the string of her bodice. The garment slipped from her injured shoulder, and her breast, like a dark full moon, was revealed. She froze for a moment.

Her father-in-law breathed deeply. 'This is dangerous,' he said eventually, in a rough whisper, 'very dangerous.' He reached out and pulled her bodice in place. Bhaunri felt his fingers tremble against her skin as he tied the strings in a knot.

'I should touch your feet for your kindness today,' she said, her bold eyes lowered.

'Better not touch any part of me right now, Chhori,' he replied.

Bhaunri looked at him out of the corner of her eye and headed towards the house.

12

OUTWARDLY, THE HOUSEHOLD REMAINED unchanged, the routines unvaried, but there was a shift, an undercurrent that altered the flow. Mai felt it and became uneasy. She spent long hours praying, promising sweetmeats to various deities and making vows in exchange for everything going well in the household. Only Bheema remained unaware, spending his days away from home, and sometimes the nights too.

'There are herds of nilgai roaming around the village. I am going hunting tonight,' he said after dinner one day, as he cleaned his gun.

Bhaunri went to the kitchen and wrapped some bread, butter and green chillies in a bit of cloth. 'I will wait for you,' she said and handed it to him.

'No need to make such preparations. I am not going on a long journey,' he said, tucking away the cloth bundle in his bag.

'When will you be back?'

'Tomorrow morning.'

'What? The whole night out in the cold forest? Who hunts like that?'

'I won't hunt the whole night. I will sleep at the Khateek's after the hunt is over.' Bheema counted under his breath as he filled a cloth bag with pellets. 'It is closer. And if I make a kill, her father can help me gut and skin the animal.'

Bhaunri pressed her lips together and said nothing in reply, but her eyes followed him until he left the house.

BHAUNRI STOPPED SINGING, braiding her hair, or lining her eyes with kohl. She went about the house, silent as a shadow. She became careless in other ways too, forgetting to untie the calf and leave him near the cow to feed, salting the dal twice, letting the milk boil over.

'What is the matter with you, daughter-in-law? Where is your head these days?' Mai said with mild exasperation one day, as they peeled kachari for drying. 'This is the fourth time you have tossed away the fruit instead of the skin.'

Bhaunri remained silent for a moment, then said, 'Mai, it is hurting beyond my bearing.'

'No, it isn't,' Mai replied with unusual sharpness. 'A woman's capacity to bear is unending – like the earth's. It is not our place to complain. Whatever fate dispenses, we have to bear. Nothing is too much.'

Bhaunri looked at her mother-in-law. 'Is that so, Mai? Nothing is too much?'

'Move your hands instead of your tongue, girl. We don't have time to chatter with all this fruit waiting to be peeled. If your fate is not benign, bear it in silence like the rest of us.'

Bhaunri made an effort. She focussed on household tasks from dawn to dusk, dried methi leaves and other winter herbs, cleaned the cowshed, fed the young calf by hand, plastered floors with a mixture of cow dung and straw. She took out the clothes her mother had stitched for her marriage, and wore a new bodice embroidered in bright colours and glinting with mirrors. She oiled her hair with fragrant jasmine oil and dyed her heels with a red dye. In the short winter afternoons, she winnowed grain and listened to the stories her father-in-law told her.

'I have been caught in a flood once, daughter-in-law. You cannot imagine it. So much water that the land loses its will to exist. It lies deep under the water's heaving folds. Every single life form that can't survive without water, that would die painfully if there is none, tries to escape the life-giver that has, in its excess, turned into a harbinger of death. I spent five nights and four days on a barren hill surrounded by the flood,' he began, breaking the sweet potato Bhaunri had roasted for him into two halves in order to cool it.

'Where did you see the flood, father-in-law?'

'In the east, where the women have skin like gold-leaf, and eyes long and narrow like the line of your kohl. I was young and home held no attraction for me, so I hitched a ride on a truck going east. I wanted to see the famous temple where virgins prayed naked to the Mother Goddess. But before I could reach the temple, the waters of the Brahmaputra rose, and there was nothing but the silver snakes of waves rippling as far as the eye could see. I survived on roots I dug out, and raw fish that I caught with my bare hands. This beggarly food, too, I shared with an eagle which had dropped at my feet, half-dead from exhaustion. There was not a single tree which was not submerged in the deluge, and nowhere to go except that bald peak.'

'And then what happened? How were you saved?'

The old Lohar smiled. 'A woman with gold-leaf skin came rowing in a boat made of bark and twigs and rescued me. But that is a story for another day.'

'What adventures you've had, father-in-law!'

'I exchanged my life for them, girl. It was not a bad trade.'

THE FREEZING MONTH of Paush had arrived. Bhaunri made preparations for a winter snack to celebrate the season. She cleaned and soaked lentils one night. The next morning, she ground them roughly with green chillies and whole black peppers, leaving the pot of batter standing beside the clay oven all day. The warmth made the batter rise light and sour, and the kitchen was fragrant as she fried the first batch of crisp, spongy savouries in the evening.

'What beauties! These Paush bada are better than God's nectar in this season, daughter-in-law,' her father-in-law said, entering the kitchen.

Mai quickly fetched a leaf platter and Bhaunri served him the puffed fritters along with crushed green coriander chutney. He ate appreciatively.

'Where did you learn to make these? It is not a dish from around your village.'

'My mother learnt it from a Bania family in my village. Their daughter was married in Jaipur. She brought the recipe to her parents' home when she returned to the village for her first delivery, she had such cravings for it. My mother helped with the birth and learnt it there.'

'And she very wisely taught it to you, along with the art of slitting throats!'

Bhaunri took another batch out of the sizzling oil with the skimmer and served them to him. 'And which do you prefer, father-in-law, eating my fritters or having your throat slit?' Bhaunri smiled.

'Hai Ram,' her mother-in-law said. 'Don't talk so much, daughter, you will burn the food.'

'Let her talk, let her talk. You want her to sit with her mouth stitched like you, woman? She has her share of silences in this house.'

Mai lowered her eyes and spoke softly. 'The relation between a father-in-law and daughter-in-law is one of maan, of distance and honour. People will say all kinds of things if they hear her chattering with you like this.'

'You can't hold their mouths so you will shut hers? Those idle gossipers can say what they please. I have never concerned myself with what people say.'

'But it is not just you whose honour will be tarnished by gossip, even Bheema's will. If not others, think of your own son.'

'Mai, whose honour is he upholding by camping at that woman's house night and day? His actions don't tarnish his honour, but my words do?' Bhaunri's throat constricted but her eyes remained dry. 'I am trying hard to bear the unbearable, Mai.'

Her father-in-law stared at her for a moment. Then he turned to his wife. 'Do not bring Bheema into this, wife, mark my words. If she talks a mouthful or two with me now and then, it harms no one, but if you cry about it, it will only bring trouble.'

His wife bowed her head and was silent. But she could not hold herself back long. One evening, while they fed the dogs, she spoke to Bheema.

'Your father is always at home these days,' she began timidly.

'Yes, I have heard he has stopped going to the theka and drinking with every good-for-nothing in the village. Perhaps in his old age he is finally turning a new leaf. He even got some stock for my shop the other day from a trader he knows.'

'An old parrot cannot learn new scriptures, son.'

'That may be so, Mai, but he is no longer causing trouble for you or me.'

'But it is not just the two of us we need to think about, there is Bhaunri too.'

'I am not worried about Bhaunri. She can take care of herself. Here, give Kalua another handful of food. His ribs are showing.' Mai silently ladled more dog food into the bowl he held out.

THE TURN IN the household continued to trouble Bhaunri's mother-in-law. She avoided being around when her husband and Bhaunri chatted.

'That's right, wife, that's good,' her husband said one afternoon, as she picked up the patchwork quilt she was threading and retreated towards the house, while Bhaunri roasted peanuts for him in the courtyard on a small coal brazier. 'You have our daughter-in-law all day long. This short hour is for me. Go inside and rest for some time.'

On hearing these words, she paused at the entrance of the house for a moment and turned to look at her husband who crouched near Bhaunri.

'Take care, father-in-law, do not provoke her. I know she was speaking to Bheema the other evening about you being at home during his absence.'

'So what if she speaks to Bheema? And what is it to anyone if I am home? I am the owner of this house, I can come and go, stay and leave as I please.'

'So you aren't afraid of Bheema's anger if she fills his ears? You know how he loathes you. He will believe the worst. He might even challenge you to a fight.'

'Am I to be afraid of that chit of a boy, daughter-in-law? Just as he does not have the brains to understand his good fortune in getting you for a wife, he does not have the brawn to fight me. Until a few years ago, I used to beat him whenever he talked back, and he would go around for days with a swollen face and a black eye.'

'What are you saying, father-in-law? That must have been a long time ago. He is a champion wrestler now. No one has defeated him in wrestling matches for years. Everyone says he knows more moves than any other wrestler around.'

'And I have forgotten more moves than he has ever learnt. I was a better wrestler than him when I was his age, and still am.'

'If Mai hadn't told me that you were famous for your skills in ten villages when you brought her home, I would have thought you were boasting. She said you used to know many special moves but gave up wrestling after you broke someone's neck in a bout. That was many years ago, she said. Perhaps you have forgotten all those moves by now.'

'Forgotten? Can a man forget how to blink? The older the banyan tree, the stronger it is. I remember every daanv and paintara I was taught by my teachers, and I can still apply all of them.'

'Really? Mai said you used to know moves to throw your opponent over your shoulder or paralyse them for a few moments. That sounded like sorcery to me!'

'Your Mai knows nothing. I not only know the move to paralyse a person for a few minutes, I also know one to paralyse someone for life without shedding a drop of blood.'

'I don't believe you, father-in-law. How can that be true? Now I am beginning to doubt all the stories you have told me.'

'Not a speck of untruth. May my favourite bullock die if I am telling a lie.'

Bhaunri curved her lips mockingly. 'But it must be a very difficult move then, one that requires much strength, skill and preparation and, therefore, can't be demonstrated, isn't it?'

'Not at all. It is not difficult. All that is needed is the knowledge of where to strike, and the right opportunity.

There is a nerve at the base of the spine. If you press it, the person will be unable to move his limbs momentarily. And if you press it very hard or damage it, the opponent is paralysed for life.'

'I don't believe you! Something like that is not possible. How can you tell such stories, father-in-law?'

'You witch, you doubt me?' He grabbed her arm and Bhaunri scrambled to her feet. The peanuts crackled and jumped in the pan over the fire. The old Lohar turned her around with a jerk of his arm and swiftly placed his broad hands on her waist. Bhaunri felt the pressure of his rough thumbs just below the long furrow of her spine. Instantly, she felt all strength drain out from her body. She would have fallen over, had her father-in-law not caught her in his arms. 'Now you made me hurt you, daughter-in-law. You have a tongue that can raise blisters.' He lowered her on to Bheema's cot. Opening Bhaunri's mouth gently, he poured drops of water from a brass tumbler, massaging her throat to help her swallow.

'I only pressed lightly. You will be all right in a few moments. A blow at this same point would cause instant paralysis for life. Now do you believe me? Or shall I show you the real move too?'

Bhaunri eyes were fixed on him. She was unable to move or speak, as if her body was caught in an invisible trap. After a few moments, she felt the locks of the trap relax. She moved her sluggish tongue in her mouth. 'I believe you...' she said in a voice like the rustling of maize ears. 'I believe everything...' Her eyes never left him.

He bent over her and touched her face, her neck, her breasts. Slowly, his warm, broad hand slid below her navel and felt the throbbing there. He crouched over her, his body enveloping hers. Bhaunri placed her arms around him, her hands moved over his back. Suddenly and soundlessly, he collapsed over her.

Bhaunri burst out laughing. 'I am a quick learner, am I not, father-in-law? That was the right nerve, wasn't it?' she said between peals of laughter. The old man looked at her helplessly as her laughter soared. 'What's that saying, father-in-law, the one about the teacher being jaggery but the disciple turning out to be the finest sugar? Isn't that true for us?'

She tried to shift his heavy body to one side as she giggled uncontrollably and knocked over the heavy brass tumbler placed by the side of the cot. The loud clatter and Bhaunri's laughter brought her mother-in-law outside. She stood frozen at the sight of her husband lying entangled with Bhaunri.

'For shame!' Her voice trembled and her eyes filled with tears. 'You are like father and daughter. At least have some shame...'

Bhaunri managed to wriggle out from under her father-in-law, who was struggling to turn over. She helped him turn and smoothed his jhagga and dhoti.

'If we are like father and daughter, my mother-in-law, then where is the question of shame?'

'Fathers don't cavort with their grown-up daughters, Bhaunri. There is decorum in every relationship. Did your mother leave behind all her shame when she left her husband for the man she lives with? Is that why she was unable to teach you any?'

Bhaunri turned the pale fire of her eyes on her mother-in-law. 'Don't talk to me of shame, Mai. My mother taught me about the marriage of hearts, without which any union is shameful. But what did you teach your son? Did you not teach him the shame of lying with every dirty prostitute? Did you not teach him the shame of breaking his wife's heart? My shame comes to me from him. It grows more piercing every day.' She held the tumbler to her father-in-law's lips. He drank a mouthful and sat up. Bhaunri picked up the winnowing fan. 'There is no cause for shame here. Father-in-law showed me a wrestling move and I tried it on him. That is all. A blind man only sees darkness everywhere.' She began winnowing millet and clearing the husk from the tiny, round grains.

Mai said nothing. She turned and went inside the house. Bhaunri's father-in-law rose wearily.

'Now are you afraid, father-in-law?' Bhaunri asked, keeping her eyes on the grain she was cleaning.

13

MAI STAYED IN HER room the whole day. Bhaunri went about the household chores by herself. She pounded bajra in the large wooden mortar which stood in a corner of the courtyard. The house resounded with the blows of the pestle as she raised and brought down her arms again and again.

After the evening milking, she set a pot of water with a measure of the broken bajra and a handful of green lentils on the clay oven to cook. She added a large helping of ghee, salt and turmeric, and carefully arranged the wood so the heat was just enough for the porridge to simmer slowly.

She passed her mother-in-law's room as she went to the storehouse to fetch jaggery. Mai was lying on a bare string cot, her hair undone, her arm across her eyes, as if she were in a house of mourning. She stood gazing at her for a moment, then said softly, 'Aren't some things beyond bearing, Mai? But love is bigger than the biggest trouble it causes. You should believe that. That is the only way to bear the unbearable.'

Mai did not stir. She lay there on the rough cot, blind and mute. Bhaunri went back to the kitchen. She was grinding garlic and red chillies into a thick paste when her father-in-law returned.

'Bajra khichdi,' he sniffed. 'The first this season. Where is your mother-in-law?'

Bhaunri pointed towards the room beyond the kitchen and, lifting the lid off the pot, added more ghee to it. The kitchen filled with fragrant warmth as steam from the pot escaped.

'Perhaps it is better this way,' he said, watching Bhaunri ladle the khichdi on to his platter. 'Let her lie in silence. I might lose my temper if she nags me today.'

Bhaunri broke a large piece of jaggery and placed it in his platter beside the khichdi. 'She might not be so silent when Bheema returns.'

'The Khateek has gone to the town to buy buffaloes. Bheema closed shop early today. Since he is not home yet, he must have gone there.' With a glance at Bhaunri, he added, 'I wish you wouldn't take it so, girl. Everyone does it in their time.'

Bhaunri did not answer and replenished his platter.

Her father-in-law rose after finishing his meal. 'You are a fire-flower, daughter-in-law, burning yourself, burning others. Anyway, he will not return this evening. At least there will be peace.' He went out into the courtyard.

He was wrong.

Shortly afterwards, the street-door opened and Bheema entered. Bhaunri heard his steps and increased the heat under the pot of khichdi. He came into the kitchen, trailing smells of earth and flesh.

'The only thing better than bajra khichdi on a cold night is you, Chhori!'

'I am not as easy to swallow as the porridge, Baalam,' Bhaunri replied.

Bheema laughed, 'You are tart like this garlic chutney. Where is Mai?'

'She is in her kothari. Won't come out and hasn't had a morsel to eat the whole day.'

'Why? Is she not well?'

'She won't look at me or speak to me.'

Bheema frowned. 'That does not sound like Mai. Something must be the matter.'

'Eat. The khichdi will get cold. Then you can ask her yourself.'

Bheema sat down, but the frown did not leave his face. 'It must be him, the pret. He must have done something.'

Bhaunri crushed a lump of jaggery between her two hands and sprinkled it over Bheema's khichdi. 'Perhaps. Now eat quickly before this becomes cold.'

'I saw him pulling on his hookah when I came in. Mai told me he has been at home a lot these days. He usually doesn't stay this long, he idles around for a few weeks and is off again. He must be up to something.'

Bhaunri remained silent, replenishing his platter with food. When he finished, he rinsed his mouth and rose. He sat smoking his chillum on the house-steps as Bhaunri wrapped up work in the kitchen. Presently, he got up and went inside.

'Bring me some coal for the hookah,' Bhaunri's father-in-law called from the courtyard.

Bhaunri picked out a few burning coals from the oven with a pair of iron tongs. She heaped them in a brass bowl and carried them out to the courtyard.

Bheema erupted out of the house behind her. 'You bastard,' he screamed. 'Don't you have enough women that you dared touch mine? I will show you this time, I will show you...'

The old Lohar continued to arrange the coals in his hookah. 'Son, it is you who can't seem to get enough women. You have a woman here worth more than all in this village and beyond, and you go looking elsewhere.'

'Don't you talk about my wife, you rabid dog! That is between her and me. I will settle with her separately.'

'If you are so jealous about her honour, don't go sticking your pathetic little thing in every dirty opening like some mongrel dog. Now shut up and let me smoke in peace.'

'When I am done with you, you won't be able to breathe, let alone smoke,' Bheema bellowed. He plucked the hookah out of his father's hands and kicked it across the courtyard. Burning embers scattered everywhere. One lodged in the string cot under the mango tree. The dry jute began to smoulder.

Bhaunri watched as her father-in-law rose and stood to face his son. 'You whelp, how dare you touch my hookah?'

'How dare you touch my woman?'

The old Lohar's fist suddenly darted and Bheema staggered. 'You should know better than to pick a fight with me. Back off now.' Bheema roared with rage and hit out wildly. His father dodged the blow and grabbed him in an iron embrace. 'You are my son, otherwise I would have broken your neck for this foolishness.'

Mai came running out of the house, her headscarf and hair dishevelled. 'Bheema,' she cried, 'don't fight with your father, my son. She is a faithless woman. If not him, it would have been someone else. Look at her, even now she stands brazenly. She has no shame. Let your father go...'

'You blame me, Mai? If he can go anywhere and do as he pleases, am I to mourn alone? If he pierces my soul, I won't let him go unscathed.'

'Let your father go, my son,' Mai keened, ignoring Bhaunri.

'You stay out of this, wife,' the old Lohar growled. 'You started this fire, you have brought this upon us. I will set you right once I am finished with this halfwit son of yours!'

Bheema got an arm loose and punched his father on the side of the head. His father staggered from the impact. He swung his arm wildly, catching Bheema on the chest. The breath left Bheema's lungs with a sound like the wind in a thorn-tree. Spluttering, he opened his mouth to gulp air.

Bhaunri ran across to where the large mortar stood and picked up the wooden pestle. She hovered around the struggling pair waiting for an opening, then, with a sudden, lightning-quick movement, she brought it down.

For a moment, Bheema stood swaying. Then his legs buckled and, wordlessly, he pitched forward. Bhaunri threw the pestle aside and caught him in her arms. She gently lowered him to the ground.

Mai rushed forward. 'Oh what have you done, daughter-in-law? You have killed him, you have killed him...'

'No, Mai, he is alive.' Bhaunri caressed Bheema's face and smiled into his staring eyes.

Her father-in-law bent over the prone body of his son and placed his ear to his chest, moved his arms and legs. 'She is right, he isn't dead. But do you realize what you have done, daughter-in-law? He is paralysed, probably for life...'

'Now he will stay at home always, now he belongs to me. Don't worry, Mai, I will take care of all his needs. I will feed him and bathe him. My heart is melded to his, there's nothing I won't do for him ... I told you, love is bigger than all troubles.'

Turning to her father-in-law she said, 'Help me carry him in.

Acknowledgements

That this book got written and published is due to those who supported me in various ways in my solitary and self-doubt filled pursuit: friends Som, Manish, Siddhartha, Gunjan who encouraged, believed and advised with astonishing generosity; Priti Gill and Ravi Singh who showed faith in my writing at an early stage; my editor Rahul Soni, without whose advice and encouragement neither *Daura* nor *Bhaunri* would have taken their present form; my publisher Udayan Mitra, whose warmth and engagement made the journey from manuscript to published book memorable; my father Dr Surendra Upadhyay, who gave me all my words, and mother Puja Upadhyay, who gave all of herself; my father-in-law and mother-in-law, Krishan Kumar Sharma and Girija Sharma, my sister, sisters-in-law, brothers-in-law, nieces, nephews, cousins, who created an affectionate and nurturing environment; my husband Vikas and son Yashodhar, who enhance me in ways I cannot describe. Towards all of them, my gratitude is unbounded, inexpressible, wordless.